Chapter One

Jim was a worrier. He worried about school, he worried about home, he even worried about what he was going to have for dinner. It wasn't a very happy life for Jim, but then he didn't know anything else: his parents were worriers too. His mother was always panicking about something. Often it was to do with whether they would have enough money or not, but it expanded to all parts of family life. 'Watch out for that car!' she would cry out to Jim, even if the car was the size of an ant on the horizon; 'make sure you put your shoes on!' was another, if Jim mentioned he was considering going to play with his friends. If they took a day trip somewhere the car journey would be filled with prophecies of doom, about the weather, about finding a car-parking space or somewhere to eat; on the way home it was similar, with Jim's mum producing a list of all of the things that had gone wrong in the day, even if it had all been fairly pleasant.

Jim's dad was also a worrier, but would never talk about it, often burying his head behind a newspaper in the evening to avoid conversation. This made for a rather explosive combination with Jim's mum, who would constantly pour her fears into Jim's dad's ears like a witch mixing a nasty potion in a cauldron. Eventually Jim's dad, carrying all of these worries in him like a volcano full of lava, would erupt, and an argument between them would begin.

This was what Jim worried about the most, though he tried to hide it, even from himself. He would go to his bedroom, close the door, sit in a corner and read a book. This was his escape route. Yes, he had a computer and games to play on it, and he did from time to time, but that was only really fun with his brother, who was older and often out a lot of the time. Reading was his real pleasure, a type of magic that transported him anywhere in any time. He lived through all sorts of adventures: a boy attending a school for wizards, orphans running away from home, small people finding powerful rings in a fantasy world. All these things could happen while his parents, downstairs, exhausted from their argument about changing a lightbulb (though it wasn't really about changing a lightbulb, it was really about something else), had gone their separate ways for a little while and mum would shout up the stairs to say that dinner was ready. Jim would go downstairs, feeling the old argument hanging in the air like weights around his neck, and the whole family would eat their dinner in silence.

It was no surprise then, that when the summer holidays came to an end and it was time to get things organised for starting high school in September, Jim was feeling very worried. Obviously most children were worried, of course they would be, but for Jim it was much worse because he came from a family of worriers. Those last few precious nights of the summer holidays were filled with panic and sleeplessness. Jim would toss back and forth, shifting pillows and duvet one way or another without success. However he positioned himself, he could not sleep. Too many unknowns about what was to come filled his mind, and his imagination, so powerful from all that reading, made them bigger and bigger and bigger. In his mind he saw himself wandering around infinite corridors, never able to find his way. He saw himself being yelled at by a teacher for not doing his homework on time, even though he found all the tasks too difficult to understand. He saw himself trapped in the changing rooms by some boys intent on turning him upside down and flushing his head down the toilet. All these were the horrors that other children in his class at primary school had told him, information gained from older brothers and sisters. One boy, Jamie Warren, had terrified Jim with a story provided by his sister; apparently, when you made it to year eight (if you made it to year eight), you had to have an injection in your arm with six needles all at once! His sister, Jamie said, still had the scar.

With the entire summer holiday ahead of him, Jim had forgotten all about these tales of terror, but now, with only a few days left before the nightmare began for real, he could not stop thinking about them. He decided to consult his brother, John, who had been at high school for two years already. Of course, he came from a family of worriers, and this meant they invested more energy in worrying about things than being open about their feelings. Jim spent some time in his own bedroom debating how best to approach the issue with his brother before crossing the landing to knock on his bedroom door.

'Come in,' he heard John say through the door. He opened it to see his brother sitting on the bed, playing a football manager game on his laptop. 'Alright?'

'Yeah,' said Jim hastily. 'I was just wondering, cos some of my mates haven't got any older brothers or sisters and they were asking, what's high school like?'

His brother continued to play his game. 'It's alright,' he said, not looking away from the screen.

Jim stood in the doorway silently, unsure whether he was satisfied with the answer or not. Occasionally his brother clicked his mouse or tapped on the keyboard, seemingly engrossed. He decided to ask another question, to probe a little further. 'Do they really flush your head down the toilet?'

John snorted a quick laugh while continuing to look at the screen. After a moment he said 'naa, that's all a load of rubbish they tell you in primary school to scare you.' He paused the game and turned to face Jim. 'It's alright you know. You get used to it pretty quickly. They show you around and stuff so you don't get lost.' He gave a brief but reassuring smile and went back to his game. This was John. Jim knew he could rely on him for sound advice and honesty. They had lived through their parents' explosive arguments together.

'Ok cool, cheers,' Jim said, and left the room. He felt a bit more at ease. He could trust his brother and was happier knowing he would be at the school too, if he needed him. He was still anxious, but not as much as before. The wild fantasies, like captured beasts, had relented from taunting him, for now.

One night, in the week before school started, Jim's mum made Jim's favourite meal, fish pie. It was crammed full of fish, peas and creamy sauce, and there were thick layers of mash potato with crunchy melted cheese on top. Jim could eat plateful after plateful without any complaint. He loved the softness of the mash next to the crunchiness of the cheese and the different textures of the fish below. Jim's mum was a great cook, and he quite liked the idea of trying it for himself; he remembered baking with his mum when he was younger, but even in the kitchen she could be stressed, and with hot pots and pans it didn't always feel like a safe place to be.

After dinner Jim's mum laid his school uniform out on his bed. 'Put this on and come downstairs so I can take a photo.' She was obsessed with taking photos. Jim wasn't sure why.

In despair, he stared down at the clothes he would have to wear most days for the next year. It didn't have the fun light blue colours of his old primary school uniform; it was darker, less colourful, more serious. There was a tie as well, black with yellow stripes. He had no idea how to put it on properly. Something else to worry about, he thought.

As Jim made his way downstairs, clad in new uniform, he felt like a clown. Everything was much too big for him. His sleeves hid his hands, his trousers drooped down around his ankles. The tie was a mess. Jim had tried to use a similar method to tying shoelaces, so that it ended up looking like a bizarre bow tie.

'You'll grow into the clothes Jim,' said his mum. He wasn't sure how long that would be. 'Clive, can you help him do his tie?' Jim's dad lowered his newspaper and looked up over his reading glasses.

'Ok,' he said, 'let's go and do your tie.' And off they went to stand in front of the hallway mirror. Over, under, over, under, round, through, tuck. Jim had no idea. He practised and practised, but every time he did it he worried about getting it wrong. He imagined himself having to do it in the changing rooms with all the other boys watching him and he kept getting confused. 'Don't worry,' his dad said. 'You'll get there in the end,' and wandered back to his newspaper.

Jim looked in the mirror and frowned. He tore off the tie in frustration. 'I'm going to bed,' he called as he walked up the stairs.

'What about the photo?' His mum shouted from the living room.

'Do it in the morning! I might have grown a bit more by then!''

Jim slammed his bedroom door shut, took off his clothes and threw them in a pile on the floor. He climbed into bed and grumbled himself to asleep.

Chapter Two

In the last days before the beginning of school, Mum made an excellent effort to spend time with Jim and John. She took them to the Shard in London and they visited Norwich Castle; considering mum was such a worrier, the days were generally a success. Jim loved visiting castles particularly because it suited his imagination. He could picture himself living a thousand years ago, when there was no such thing as high school.

Sadly, however, the dreaded first day drew closer and Jim's worry increased. For all their problems, his family were a loving bunch and they did their best to ease his troubled thoughts. First came Dad, knocking on the door while Jim was packing his school bag. He said 'your mother has asked me to take you to school in the morning on my way to work. I can drop you off just round the corner.'

'Great, thanks Dad,' Jim said, trying to sound thankful rather than worried.

Next it was Mum. She came in and said 'I've turned your trousers up Jim. They should fit you properly now.'

'That's great, thanks Mum,' Jim said, trying not to sound ungrateful because his jumper was still far too big for him.

Finally came John with a solution to Jim's biggest concern of all – the tie.

'Here, try this,' John said, chucking something at him. It was his school tie, pre-tied with a perfect knot. The only problem was that the hole to put his head through was far too big: the tie knot would hang some way down his chest.

'Er… Thanks John,' he said questioningly.

'Put it over your head,' his brother replied. 'Hold the knot and pull the thin bit.' Jim did what he was told and the knot moved up to his neck without getting smaller or tighter. 'There you go,' said John. 'Now you won't have to worry about tying it up after PE. Just slide it on and slide it back off again. I did that the whole way through year seven.'

Jim put on the tie and was satisfied. He slid the knot up and down several times and found it very easy to use. 'Cheers bruv,' he said.

The hours of the last day seemed to slip through his fingers and soon it was time for bed. He did not sleep very well. His mind was racing with bizarre dreams of toilets chasing after him and giant eight-pronged needles. He woke several times in the night, worried that he might be late, so that when he finally did get to sleep he overslept. His first day of school started with a sudden awakening caused by the panicked entrance of his father into his bedroom. 'Come on boy, I've got to leave in twenty minutes and you're not even up yet!'

Oh no, thought Jim. This was a bad start.

'Clive, calm down,' he heard his mum say from downstairs. 'It's his first day!'

'I know, but I've got to get to work!' his dad replied in a raised voice.

He leapt out of bed and rushed downstairs for a quick bowl of cereal, stubbing his toe on a step on the way before hopping around the hallway in agony. Foot nursed and cereal eaten in record time, Jim accelerated back upstairs to the bathroom where he quickly washed his face and brushed his teeth and hair. Next he dived into his bedroom to get dressed; he could hear his dad revving the car on the drive outside. Pants, socks, shirt, tie, jumper and trousers (perhaps a little too short now). Once more he shot downstairs, gave a hurried goodbye to his mother as he put on his shoes and raced out the door to his dad's car, where he and John were waiting.

'Right, let's go,' his dad said, and off they went. The journey to school did not take very long and, after panicking about being late, he found that his dad had dropped them off incredibly early so that he could get to work on time (his father always worried about being late to work). The playground at the front of the school was notably empty and only a couple of other innocent year sevens loitered in its lonely corners.

Seconds after their father's car roared away, his brother said something that made Jim's heart sink. 'Where's your bag?' What a disaster! In his rush to get to the car, Jim had forgotten to pick up his school bag. John noticed the look of horror on his face. 'Here,' he said, passing Jim a pen. 'I can lend you this today. Should be all you need.' Good old John, saving the day once more. 'Now, you need to wait here, I've got to go to the other playground for older pupils. Have a good day,' he said, giving Jim a reassuring smile which he tried, and failed, to copy. He looked around him at the other year sevens and couldn't build the courage to go and speak to them. He simply stood there in his corner and became another lonely statue waiting for the time to pass.

Eventually others arrived, some boys from his primary school, and he went and stood with them. The first to arrive, Greg, had always been annoying in primary school, stealing pens and making fun whenever possible. Now was no exception. He began laughing at Jim for forgetting his school bag on the first day. As each new boy from his primary school arrived, Greg insisted on announcing Jim's blunder. 'Oi Jamie, guess what Jim's done. Forgotten his school bag HAHAHA!'

Nobody else found it as funny as Greg and mostly the boys were sympathetic, but nonetheless his constant going-on about it made Jim even more anxious. He didn't want everyone to know. 'Oh shut UP Greg!' He shouted after Greg had told Todd, the fifth boy to arrive, about Jim's bag. Greg, not wanting to appear weak in front of any of the boys on the first day, turned on Jim and shoved him to the ground. 'What are you going to do about it Jim?'

A couple of other boys pulled Greg away and he went off to see a friend who had just arrived. Jim scrambled to his feet. Great, he thought, I've been here five minutes and I've already got into a fight.

Eventually the bell went and he started the school day properly. He met the rest of his form group, who seemed nice enough, though by some unlucky circumstance he was in the same group as Greg. It appeared that he had not forgiven him for earlier in the day and often Jim would look up to find Greg giving him evil looks. Jim thought about telling his form tutor, Mr Kelly, who was a very cheerful and friendly man, but was too worried about the consequences. Besides, what could really be done about one pupil looking at another?

Mr Kelly took the pupils through their timetables and talked through the rules and expectations in lessons. This worried Jim even more. It seemed as if the whole system was set up to punish the pupils. One rule after another after another, all of which resulted in a detention if broken. Jim could feel the blood draining from his face when Mr Kelly mentioned that a detention would be given for forgetting equipment.

'Sir!' shouted Greg from somewhere at the back of the class. 'Jim has forgotten his equipment today sir!'

Mr Kelly stared at him. 'Greg, do you remember what I said about calling out?'

'Yes, sir,' Greg replied, looking at his table and trying to appear humble.

'Well don't forget it,' Mr Kelly said. 'Have you forgotten your equipment Jim?'

Jim at this point was horrified into speechlessness. He had hoped he would have been able to avoid saying anything in class for his entire time at school, and here he was on his first day being asked a direct question from the teacher. Even worse, it was about something he had done wrong. He could feel everyone looking at him and he could hear the silence humming in the air. He wanted to say something but no words came. In the end he resorted to a nod. Mr Kelly, some sympathy appearing in his eyes, said 'OK, today is your first day, so we'll let you off,' Greg looked up in indignation, 'just like I let off Greg for calling out just now,' Greg looked back down. 'Make sure you bring it tomorrow.' Jim nodded vigorously.

The rest of the day was both tiresome and scary in equal measure. After spending one lesson with Mr Kelly, he had English, then maths, then French, but rather than learning anything about those subjects, the teachers just repeated what had already been said in the first lesson. They all had stern expressions on their faces and Jim wondered why they bothered to do the job at all when they hated it so much.

Finally, however, the school day ended: Jim had made it through unscathed. He should have felt relieved, but there was still the journey home to think about. Originally Jim was going to walk with his older brother, but circumstances had changed. John, it seemed, had got a new girlfriend and wanted to walk home with her. 'Sorry, Jim, but you know the way, don't you?' John said. Jim nodded and gulped as he watched his brother walk off in the other direction.

The route home was a worry. He had to take a narrow claustrophobic path that had high fences on either side. It began with a steep descent, followed by a sharp corner at the bottom which was supposed to be a popular waiting place for bullies and criminals. Older children from the high school called it Black Hill. To make matters worse, among the stories Jamie Warren had told in primary school was the one about the old woman who lived at the bottom of the hill. Apparently she came out at the end of the school day to shout at pupils who walked across her front lawn. Jamie's mum had called her a witch because she put curses on people; the witch's son, according to Jamie's mum, was a drug addict, struggling to deal with his mother's wicked ways. For Jim this was too much, enough to make him walk any other way. But it was the quickest route home, and, after a long day at school, the sooner he reached the refuge of his bedroom the better.

He began to walk down the path and it was indeed steep. There was graffiti on the fence all the way down and this made Jim even more nervous. People, he thought, commit crimes down here. Even though it was the afternoon it seemed dark along the path. Trees from the neighbouring gardens hung over the fences and blocked out a lot of the light. Jim began to walk faster. He made it to the halfway point when he heard the sound of boys talking at the top of the hill. He decided not to turn around and carried on, but someone called from behind.

'Hey Jim!'

He turned and, to Jim's horror, the voice belonged to none other than Greg. 'I want you to meet my brother and his friends.' A menacing smile spread across Greg's face as three larger boys emerged behind him.

'Er, I'm alright thanks Greg, I've gotta get back home,' Jim shouted nervously, turning around and increasing his pace without bothering to hear what Greg had to say. But Jim's reply did not deter the boys, and in an instant he heard running footsteps behind him. Jim began to run too; he reached the bottom of the hill and turned the sharp corner. The boys were not far behind him; he could hear them laughing; one shouted 'we're going to get you!'

Panicking, Jim sprinted out of the bottom of the alleyway and into the avenue, but, turning his head to see how far away the boys were, he tripped and keeled over on the grass. Now he was in for it. He could hear the boys coming out of the alley and there was no time for him to do anything; he couldn't run, he couldn't even get up in time. Soon they would be upon him. Oh no, thought Jim, this is everything I feared.

Then something bizarre happened. The boys seemed to ignore Jim completely. Instead they turned left and walked off in the opposite direction. It was as if they had forgotten they were even chasing him. Not wanting to draw their attention back to him, Jim stayed lying on the ground, but rolled over onto his elbow to watch them walk off in disbelief. When they were out of sight, Jim was just about to heave a sigh of relief when he heard a door open. Looking behind him, he realised he was not just on any patch of grass, he was on someone's front lawn. And that someone was not just anyone, it was the old woman, the witch, surely come to put a curse on him. It was too late though; he had no time to do anything.

She stood in the open doorway and stared at Jim. She was dressed in brown shoes, smart grey trousers and a purple jumper. She wore large round glasses that matched her rotund figure and had big, curly, grey hair. She leaned some weight on a walking stick in her left hand. And she stared. Jim would have stood up and got off her lawn immediately, except he was so scared he couldn't move.

'You're welcome,' said the woman, strangely, and she smiled. She spoke with an accent that Jim didn't recognise, but someone more worldly would have guessed she was from Cornwall.

Jim scrambled to his feet, stepped off the lawn and brushed himself down in quick succession. 'I'm sorry I fell on your lawn,' he said, the words moving so quickly out of his mouth they were almost tripping up over each other to escape.

The woman just looked at him and smiled. 'Would you like to come in for a cup of tea?'

What a strange question! Was this what the old woman did – invite lonely pupils into her house and then cook them like some story in a fairy tale? Surprisingly, there was something inside Jim that was keen for him to say yes, as if something were calling him into the house. But sensible Jim, fearful Jim, knew better. 'No thanks,' he said, trying to smile.

'Oh well,' said the old woman. 'Maybe tomorrow.' And she closed the door.

Jim walked home at a much quicker pace than usual. When he finally made it to his bedroom and closed the door, he heaved a sigh of relief. Would every school day be filled with so much stress and worry?

Chapter Three

The next day Jim was so worried about getting up late for school that he barely slept. He kept his bag ready in front of his bedroom door so that he would have to pick it up to leave.

He was up before his dad this time, and had plenty of time to eat his breakfast and have a proper wash (whatever that might be for an eleven year old boy). When his dad finally came down the stairs, Jim was already dressed and ready to go.

'Alright boy,' his dad said. 'I'll be ready in a minute or two.'

Jim quite liked this way of doing things. It meant that he could relax and watch cartoons while his dad was eating breakfast, and cartoons were a lot like reading. They were a safe place where Jim could completely forget about the rest of the world.

But the time to watch television went all too quickly and Jim was soon in the car with his dad and brother. As they set off, Jim noticed something different to the day before. 'What's that smell, Dad?'

Dad took a deep breath in, then lots of short sharp sniffs. He made a big deal of trying to identify the smell, eventually leaning in John's direction. He said 'are you wearing my cologne John?'

John went a deep red colour. 'I think the smell is John, Jim. I reckon he is trying to impress somebody,' Dad said, and gave Jim a wink.

'No I'm not, shut up Dad,' replied John, folding his arms and looking out the window. Jim chuckled, and John gave him a quick clip round the back of the head.

Dad dropped them off at school just as early as the day before and the playground was empty once again. Gradually people arrived and some boys from his old primary school came and stood with him. It was strange how this happened. Only one of them, Tom, did Jim consider to be his friend. They had been friends for years and often Jim would go to Tom's house to play computer games on a Saturday afternoon. Yet all of the boys from his primary school stood together now, friend or not, having nothing better to do.

Greg arrived with his brother and Jim began to panic that there would be a repetition of the previous day's events, but thankfully they ignored him. Greg went with his brother to the playground for older pupils and Jim felt incredibly relieved. In fact, Greg seemed to ignore him all day, and, apart from a lesson with a rather intimidating maths teacher, Jim had a fairly painless day.

At the end of school Jim hurried to leave. He saw his brother leaving with the girl who was supposed to be his girlfriend and realised he would have another lonely walk home. As he reached the top of Black Hill he was worried once more about some altercation with Greg and his brothers, but thankfully no one appeared. He was cautious as he walked down the hill and turned the corner, but when he came out of the alleyway and realised he was free, he felt an enormous lightening of worry.

He walked past the lawn that he fell on the day before and realised as he did so that he was being watched. The door of the old woman's house was open again and there, curly grey hair, round glasses and walking stick, she stood. She smiled at Jim, but he couldn't work out whether it was friendly or not. He decided to walk by.

'You're welcome,' she said, which Jim thought was a funny thing to say. Then he remembered that she had said the exact same thing the day before. In a moment of curiosity, he decided to respond.

'What for?' he said, turning around.

'Those boys. They've stopped bothering you, haven't they?'

'Err, yeah, they have,' Jim replied.

'Well,' said the old woman, 'you're welcome.'

'I don't understand. Why am I welcome?'

'Because I stopped them from bothering you, and normally when someone does something nice for you, you say thank you.'

'Er...' said Jim, his mind now starting to consider the possibility that the rumours about this old woman being mad were true. 'Well, thank you.'

'You're very welcome my darling. Would you like to come in for a cup of tea now?'

While Jim could just about stomach having a conversation with the old woman on her front lawn, where they were in clear view, the thought of entering her house was different altogether. 'Ahh, no, sorry, that's very kind of you,' said Jim, doing his absolute best to be polite, 'but I really must be getting home. My mother is expecting me.'

'Suit yourself,' said the old woman, giving another smile. Then she turned around and closed the door without saying goodbye. Odd, thought Jim, but he had no time to contemplate the situation as he heard the recognisable sound of Greg and his cronies chatting as they came down Black Hill. He decided to make a swift departure back home.

The next day was Friday and it started in much the same way as the one before. Jim realised there was some comfort in routine. 'What lessons have we got today?' said Tom, who was also in the same form as Jim.

'French, science, PE and art,' Jim replied.

'Ahh yes I love PE,' said Tom.

But Jim did not love PE. He didn't mind other subjects, science, English, maths (if it wasn't for the scary teacher) because he knew if he concentrated he could quietly get a good grade. But PE was different. He wasn't that good at it, particularly team sports; he worried about the possibility of being shoved around and he worried about making a mistake and letting everyone else down. He was also worried about getting changed in the changing rooms. He would have to take his clothes off and there would be no teacher there. Someone might steal his things, or push him in the showers; a whole range of things could go wrong.

PE came lesson three, just before lunch. Boys and girls had to stand in separate queues outside the PE block before going inside to get changed. This made Jim even more nervous. Obviously he didn't want to get changed in front of the girls, but they always seemed so much nicer, calmer, more sensible, that they often prevented a lot of the boys' silliness.

The PE teacher came out and stood in front of the two queues. 'Right,' he said. 'Girls, you're going in the left door. Boys, you're going in the right. You've got five minutes to get changed and then meet in the sports hall.' He had a big smile on his face, but there was something about it that didn't seem friendly, as if he knew Jim was worried and he was happy about that.

The boys went into the changing rooms and each rushed to find a private corner. All were quiet as they took off their school uniforms and put on their new PE kits as quickly as possible. Nobody wanted to be the last one out. Jim could feel the panic rising inside when he realised he was one of four boys left. He was struggling to pull his long yellow socks up, and panicking didn't help. One by one the remaining boys left and it was just him. Finally the socks were on, he slipped on his trainers, tied them up and ran to the sports hall. As he entered, the rest of the class and the teacher stood watching silently. Jim, embarrassed, joined the back of the group.

The lesson itself was fine. They had to do something called a bleep test, which meant running the length of the sports hall over and over, trying to get to the other end before a bleep sounded on a speaker. Jim found it tiring, but he was able to stop whenever he wanted and so gave up at level seven. Tom, who was a lot fitter than Jim, made it to level eleven, the second best in the group.

Problems began back in the changing rooms. Jim had just started to get changed when a hand reached round and grabbed his school shirt from off the bench.

He turned around. It was Greg. Jim just looked at him; he wanted to say 'give it back Greg' or something similar, but the words just wouldn't come. For some reason, Jim felt a lot more scared of Greg now than when they had been in primary school. It was Tom that intervened. 'Come on Greg, give him his shirt back.'

Greg had a big smile on his face. 'I just thought it looked a little dirty, that's all,' he said. 'Thought I might give it a wash!' And on the word 'wash' Greg reached behind, holding the shirt under a running shower. He laughed moronically and then threw it back at Jim. It thudded, sodden, against his chest and then landed with a splat on the floor. Great, thought Jim.

And that was the rest of the day: sitting in a wet shirt throughout lunch and period four, covering it up with his school jumper. When the bell went for home time Jim made another speedy getaway, not even bothering to see if his brother was walking the same way too. When he got to the top of Black Hill, he looked around and, seeing that Greg was nowhere in sight, descended quickly. Hopefully, he thought, if I leave at this time every day, I can avoid him altogether. But Jim was wrong, for as he turned the corner there stood Greg, his older brother and his older brother's friend, who just happened to be putting out a cigarette as Jim appeared.

When Greg saw Jim a cruel smile grew on his face, swiftly mimicked by his two companions. 'Hello Jim,' he said. 'How nice to see you.' But Jim could tell, as anyone could, that Greg did not mean this at all.

He froze, stared at the three of them. 'Off home, Jim?' asked Greg's older brother. He could only bring himself to nod. 'Well, off you go then,' said Greg, and the three of them, still smiling, stepped out of his way to let him pass. Jim thought this might be some kind of trick, but had no intention of turning around and going the other way. There was no way he would be able to sprint up Black Hill, especially after doing the Bleep Test that day.

He walked past Greg, and nothing happened. He walked past Greg's brother, and nothing happened. He walked past Greg's brother's friend, and nothing happened. Maybe he was free. He began to walk slightly faster, but the boys, merely playing with him, now pounced on him and pushed him to the ground. One of them (Jim couldn't see who) picked up his bag and ran out of the alleyway with it. The other two followed and laughed. Jim, panicking, got up. He was torn between trying to escape the boys and trying to get his bag back. As he stepped out of the alleyway, he saw them waiting; his bag, it seemed, had been thrown onto the old woman's front lawn. Jim moved to pick it up and, as he did so, Greg jumped on him and pushed him over. 'Get him Greg!' the other boys yelled. Jim rolled over and looked up to see Greg's raised fist above his head. Any moment it would smash down onto his face. Jim was terrified.

Then, strangely, there seemed to be a change in atmosphere. 'Leave him Greg. He's not worth it,' said Greg's brother, and Greg, lowering his fist, seemed to agree with him. He stood up and the three boys walked off, laughing as they did so. Jim lay there, stunned.

A moment later the front door of the old woman's house opened. Like before, she appeared in the doorway. 'You're welcome,' she said.

'Er.. thank you,' said Jim, and this time he felt like he meant it.

'Perhaps you should come in for that cup of tea now?'

Jim, still in disbelief as to what had just happened, agreed. 'Ok,' he said, and he stood up and walked into the house.

It began with a narrow hallway. The old woman showed him into the living room, which was very much how you would expect an old person's house to look. The furniture seemed old fashioned, though clean, and there were comfortable sitting chairs all around. In the middle, resting on a table, was a pot of tea and two cups, as if she had been expecting Jim to call. He was struck by the sweet, relaxing smell that seemed to flood the air. Several bouquets of flowers, Jim realised, decorated the room. 'Take a seat,' the old woman said.

Jim sat down, still in a bit of a daze. The old woman sat opposite him, smiled, picked up the tea pot and began to pour. Neither of them spoke and the only sound was the tea tinkling into the cup and Jim's heavy breathing. 'Do you take sugar?' the old woman asked. 'No, thank you,' said Jim.

Having poured the milk the old woman handed Jim the cup, saying 'there you are.' Jim thanked her and then stared into the cup, a bit uncertain what to do with it. This happened to be Jim's first ever cup of tea. He held it tentatively with the tips of his fingers, waiting for the moment when he thought it would be cool enough to drink.

The old woman sat down in the chair opposite him, her short legs barely touching the floor. She stared at him for a moment, smiling. 'Are you alright now Jim?' she asked.

'Yes, much better thank you,' Jim said, trying to sound confident. He couldn't remember whether he had told her his name.

'My name is Mrs Florence,' she said. 'It's nice to meet you.'

'It's nice to meet you too,' said Jim in reply. Then neither of them spoke. Jim had questions but didn't feel brave enough to ask. He wasn't sure whether it would be rude for him to speak first or whether he should, as he had been told so many times when he was younger, wait until he was spoken to. He looked around the room; there were paintings hung on the walls of various coastal scenes, fishing villages, cliffs, ships at sea. There were sculptures too, a man sitting cross-legged, a crucifix and other symbols and images that Jim didn't recognise. The most significant features of the room, however, were the glorious bunches of flowers that seemed to fill every space. Beautiful colours emanated from the petals of flowers of such a range of shapes and sizes, none of which Jim knew the names.

'You're frightened, aren't you Jim?' There was something about the way she looked at him which made him feel as if she were looking right inside. Again Jim wasn't sure what the correct way to respond was. He didn't want to seem impolite by saying that he was frightened because then maybe Mrs Florence would assume that he was frightened of her.

'Yes, I am a bit,' he replied, deciding to plump for honesty. He felt himself beginning to relax and took his first sip of tea. Mrs Florence watched him and smiled at him as she did so. He decided to brave a question. 'Did you stop those boys from beating me up?'

'In a way,' Mrs Florence replied.

'How?'

'I asked.'

Jim thought about this for a moment. He couldn't remember hearing her voice as he stared up at Greg's fist. Jim didn't want to seem rude, but he was curious and so went a bit further.

'I didn't hear you ask them,' he said.

A big smile showing all of Mrs Florence's teeth broke out across her face, like the sun dawning on a new day. 'Oh my darling,' she said, her Cornish accent becoming thicker, 'I didn't ask *them*. That would have been pointless. I asked the Universe.' Jim looked puzzled. 'The Universe gives me everything I ask for,' she said simply.

'It does?' Jim asked, feeling dizzy with scepticism and confusion. He suddenly realised he was drinking tea in a strange house with a mad woman. He couldn't help but frown.

'It does,' she said, and smiled again.

'But, how?'

'Because I believe that it will.'

'Right... Well, thanks very much for the tea,' said Jim, hurrying to leave.

'You don't believe me, do you?' Mrs Florence said as Jim got up.

'Er...' Once again Jim felt honesty was best. 'Not really, no.'

'That's ok, not many people do. That's why so many of them are unhappy. Anyone can do it, but no one believes that they can.'

Jim didn't know what to say. He nodded respectfully and then said 'I really should go. My mum will be wondering what has happened to me.'

'Yes she will,' Mrs Florence agreed, and leaned on her walking stick to get up. 'Thank you for coming Jim. You are welcome any time.' She smiled that sunshine smile again and Jim felt suddenly very warm to her, regardless of her crazy ideas.

'Thanks,' he said. 'Bye.'

Mrs Florence watched him as he walked out of the house and then closed the door.

Jim couldn't help thinking about what she had said on the way home. Surely it was nonsense, he thought. You couldn't simply just ask for what you wanted and then get it. Otherwise everyone would do it. And what would be the point of life? Everyone would just be sitting around doing nothing, asking the Universe to drop some fish and chips into their laps.

Yet when Jim got home, he still couldn't stop thinking about it. After all, Greg had walked away without punching him. It didn't make sense that he would have a complete change of heart at such short notice. And was Mrs Florence saying that she could control people's actions? If that was the case why was she living in this tiny house in this boring town all by herself, doing nothing? Surely she could be mayor or something, at least. And if the Universe gave her everything she asked for, why didn't she have loads of money? Or a sports car? It must all be nonsense, mustn't it?

By some strange coincidence, Jim had fish and chips that night. He thoroughly enjoyed it and was so caught up in pondering his conversation with Mrs Florence that he didn't seem to worry about everything that had happened that day in the changing rooms. He actually quite liked her, even if he did think she was mad. She was different to his parents. He had never seen anyone smile as much. Maybe, he thought, as he was lying in bed that night, maybe I will call in for another cup of tea on Monday, just to see how she is.

Jim went to bed that night and he had a deep, satisfying sleep, perhaps the best he had had since he started high school.

Chapter Four

The next day something strange came over Jim. He decided to follow in Mrs Florence's footsteps and ask the Universe for something. He thought about it for a long time and decided to ask for a sports car. Obviously he was too young to drive it now, but, if what Mrs Florence had said was true and he did get one, maybe his mum or dad could drive him around in it until he was old enough. He stood in the bathroom and looked into the mirror while brushing his teeth. He considered how he should phrase his request, decided he would word it similar to how he might ask for a birthday or Christmas present, and then said 'Dear Universe, please can I have a brand new sports car?'

Obviously nothing happened. He looked out of the window and didn't see a sports car appear on his drive. Almost immediately he began to feel a little silly. The toothpaste froth around the sides of his mouth made him look like a bit of a circus clown. He finished brushing his teeth and cleaned his face. Oh well, he thought, maybe the Universe just needs a bit of time.

Most of the rest of the weekend was quite fun. Jim went to see Tom on Saturday afternoon and they played computer games. Then in the evening, it was one of those rare occasions in Jim's house where the family would sit together for dinner and Mum and Dad wouldn't argue. They ate Chinese takeaway (Jim loved Kung Po Chicken) and then watched some Saturday night TV. Most of Sunday was good too; Mum made a roast for lunch, which was delicious.

By the afternoon, however, Jim realised he had better do the homework that had been set the week before. He began to wonder if every Sunday afternoon would be cursed with preparing for the week ahead in this way.

Sunday evening came and Jim began to feel the dread of going back to school bubble in his stomach. Would it be this way before every Monday morning, he thought. He looked out of his window at bedtime and stared down at the drive. Still the Universe had not supplied him with a sports car. He had a dwindling hope that it might appear Monday morning, but in reality Jim knew it was never going to happen. A stupid idea inspired by a crazy old woman. Simple as that. Jim went to bed feeling foolish, disappointed and anxious about school the next day.

Monday morning came and still no sports car. Of course, thought Jim. It was all so ridiculous, he couldn't believe that he had tried it in the first place. He got to school early as usual, the playground empty as usual. The faint excitement at doing something new that existed on the faces of the other year seven boys last week was starting to fade. It was slowly becoming obvious that they would have another five years of this.

Jim had maths first lesson and was devastated when Mrs Numbers (a funny name for a maths teacher) asked everyone to get their homework out and he couldn't find it in his bag. 'That's going to have to be a detention Jim,' she said. 'I'm disappointed. This isn't a very good start at all.'

Jim couldn't believe it. He had sat and done his Maths homework yesterday afternoon and he was sure he had put it in his bag. He thought he could probably tell her what the answers to the questions were if she asked, but she wouldn't. She was a stern, fierce woman and it was clear her decision was final.

The detention was after school that day. Mrs Numbers had spoken to his mum, she had said, and he would have to stay until four o'clock to complete the work. Jim felt some satisfaction when he was able to complete it all in fifteen minutes because he had remembered it from the day before. 'That's really good Jim, well done,' said Mrs Numbers, in a tone that suggested he had misjudged her somewhat. He thought perhaps she might let him go, but instead she said 'now try this,' and handed him another worksheet. It was more of the same. Doesn't she realise I can do this already, thought Jim, why do I need to do more?

Finally the detention was over and Jim was keen to get home. After the trouble he had had with Greg and the strange conversations with Mrs Florence, he had been considering taking a different, longer route home, but now, keen to get back as soon as possible after the detention, he went down Black Hill once more. At least Greg and his group of cronies would have already gone home. He should be able to slip by Mrs Florence's house unnoticed.

When Jim came out of the alleyway at the bottom of Black Hill, however, there was Mrs Florence, standing in the doorway, as if waiting for him. She wore a purple jumper and grey trousers as usual and she was leaning on her walking stick. Jim thought about turning back, but it was too late. She had already seen him. He smiled at her, but carried on walking. As he passed her front door, he could feel her eyes looking at him. He had just gone by her when she said 'you asked for something, didn't you my darling?'

Jim stopped. He slowly turned and looked up at her. He debated telling the truth, but then decided not to. He didn't want her to think that he had fallen for her stupid stories. 'No,' he said, as firmly as possible, but then looked down, feeling the weight of his lie in his stomach.

'Yes you did. What did you ask for?'

Jim decided to give in. 'A sports car,' he said hopelessly, full of embarrassment.

'A sports car?' Mrs Florence said, a big smile coming across her face. 'Now what on earth would you want one of those for?'

'I dunno, just thought it would be cool,' said Jim, shrugging his shoulders. He felt she was making fun of him, as if he were foolish for falling for her lies and foolish for asking for such a foolish thing. But Mrs Florence's response surprised him.

'Yes, I guess it would be cool,' she said, nodding. 'Did the Universe supply?'

'No,' he said. 'No, it didn't.'

'Ahh well, would you like to come in for a cup of tea?'

'No thanks,' Jim said, 'I need to get home.'

'Ok then. Bye,' Mrs Florence said, smiling, and shut the door.

'Stupid woman with her stupid stories,' grumbled Jim to himself as he walked home. 'Made a right fool out of me. I bet she is having a right laugh in her stupid house now.'

Jim continued to be in a bad mood when he got home and Mum told him off for getting a detention. 'But Mum,' he said in protest, 'I did the homework, I did it yesterday afternoon, you saw me doing it!' Mum, however, was having none of it. She was more interested in taking the adult's side than listening to what Jim had to say. Jim stomped upstairs and went to his bedroom. There, underneath his desk, having fallen out of his bag that morning, was his Maths homework. 'Arrgh!' shouted Jim, grabbing the sheet, screwing it up and throwing it in the bin.

The next day, he was careful to pack his bag with the homework he needed, and thankfully made it through all of his lessons without receiving any detentions. His brother was still walking home with his new girlfriend (it seemed they had become quite the item) and despite the desire to take a different route home, Jim opted for ease and decided to go down Black Hill as usual. He spied Greg and his friends some distance in front of him and decided to hang back until he was sure he would not cross their path. When he got to the top of Black Hill he looked down and guessed that they must have turned the corner, for he could not see them. Had they exited the alley, or were they lurking just out of sight, aware that Jim was close behind them?

He crept down the hill slowly, listening intently for any noise that might be made. When he made it to the bottom he heard Greg say 'Wow, look at that!' Jim could tell that they had left the alleyway, so he crept round the corner and hid just out of sight behind some bushes. He could see Greg, his brother and his brother's friend looking at something in wonder, but he couldn't see what the object was.

'That is awesome,' said Greg's brother.

'Yeah, wicked,' said his friend. 'I bet it goes well quick.'

'Yeah,' said Greg.

The three boys spent a long time admiring the unknown object and Jim began to wonder whether he would be better off going back up Black Hill and taking the longer route home. Eventually, however, Greg's brother said they had better get going, and off they went. Slowly Jim emerged from the alleyway and as he did so his heart jumped into his mouth.

Sitting in front of Mrs Florence's house, next to her front lawn, was a bright orange convertible sports car. Jim couldn't believe it. He stared and stared. He couldn't find the words to speak. A sports car!

Jim had to find out what it was doing there. For the first time, he walked straight up to Mrs Florence's house and knocked. He could hear someone shuffling along the hallway behind the front door. He heard clicking as locks were undone. Jim couldn't contain himself. Please hurry up and open the door, he thought. And then she did.

'Oh, hello Jim, how nice to see you,' Mrs Florence said, a big smile forming across her face. 'How are you?'

'Yeah, I'm fine,' said Jim, perhaps a little impolitely, but he was too keen to move on to the subject that occupied his mind. 'Is that *your* sports car?'

'Oh, that,' said Mrs Florence, feigning little interest, 'yes it is.'

'But – how did – what the – why…' Jim was stuck for words.

Mrs Florence, who was only a little bit taller than Jim (and would no doubt be a lot shorter by the time he reached sixteen), leaned forward, looked Jim right in the eye and said 'I *asked*, Jim.' She turned around and walked into the living room, leaving the front door open. Jim saw it as an invitation to follow, which he duly did.

'But, how come you get a sports car and I don't!' he said, desperate to know the secret.

Mrs Florence looked up slowly. 'Have you closed the door?' Jim shook himself, as if he had just remembered his manners.

'Oh, no, sorry,' he said, and rushed back to close it. He carefully took his shoes off and left them in the porch, then walked back into the living room.

'Please have a seat,' said Mrs Florence. 'Cup of tea?'

'Yes please,' said Jim, sitting down. There was a silence while she poured the tea and Jim sat waiting, desperate for an answer.

'Patience,' said Mrs Florence, handing him a cup of tea, 'is really important.'

'Ok,' said Jim, and he decided the best thing to do was to sit in silence and blow on his drink. Mrs Florence stirred her tea and then sat back in her chair.

'So,' said Mrs Florence, 'what do you want to know?'

'Well, it's just, I ask for a sports car and wait all weekend and don't get one. But you ask and get one straight away. How come? What did I do wrong?'

Mrs Florence smiled. 'Well,' she said, 'how did you ask?'

Jim thought about it. 'I was in the bathroom, brushing my teeth, and I said "Dear Universe, please can I have a sports car?" or something like that.'

'Ok, then what did you do?'

'I didn't really do anything. Looked out the window, and got on with the rest of my weekend.'

Mrs Florence nodded and looked straight into him. 'You're a nice boy Jim. The Universe wants to work for you, as it wants to work for everyone, but you have to know how to do things properly.' She paused and looked at him. 'But, no. I don't think you really want to know this, not really.'

'Yes,' said Jim. 'I do, please.'

'No,' said Mrs Florence teasingly. 'I don't think you are ready.'

'I am, Mrs Florence, I promise,' and he tried his best to give his most convincing smile.

'Ok, but pay attention.' Jim nodded. 'First of all, when you ask the Universe for something, don't do it while brushing your teeth. If you want whatever it is you are asking for, then you need to give the proper time to ask for it; don't do it while you are doing something else.'

'Ok,' said Jim. He wasn't sure whether he was being told off or not, but there was a warmth to Mrs Florence's eyes that assured him all was well.

'Secondly,' she said, 'you have to change the way you ask. Don't actually ask; try to make it more of a demand. Something like "Dear Universe, bring me a sports car. I give thanks that it appears now." There needs to be more confidence than just asking. Or you can be even more arrogant. Something like "Dear Universe, I am the owner of a sports car. I give thanks that it appears now in the best way." Do you understand?'

'Yeah, right, think so,' said Jim, a bit puzzled. Making a demand like that seemed a little bit rude to

Jim, but he wasn't about to question the old woman. After all, she was the one with the sports car on her drive, not him.

'Finally,' said Mrs Florence, and she opened her hands to show how important her statement was. 'And this is the really important bit. You have to *believe* that it is going to happen. And not just that, you have to *show* the Universe that you believe it is going to happen. So after I asked for an orange sports car, I did a few things. First of all I went outside and I cleared my drive so that there was a space to put the car.' Jim thought about it. The drive had been full of plant pots and various other things yesterday. 'The second thing I did was I tore up my bus pass and threw it in the bin.'

'Why?'

'To show the Universe that I fully believed that it would provide me with another mode of transport. And it did. Moments later I saw an advert for a competition, which I entered and won. They delivered the sports car this morning.'

Jim couldn't quite believe it was as simple as that, and yet it was hard for him to dispute the proof. 'Is it really as easy as that?' he asked.

'No,' she replied, 'it is as hard as that. Showing active faith in the Universe is very hard to do when you start. It can be quite scary. It is a bit easier for you because you are young. It is best to start when you are young and the fears of the world haven't taken hold of you yet... Though you are a fearful one, aren't you Jim?'

But Jim felt strangely confident. He felt as if Mrs Florence had told him something completely true, something which he had been missing all his life. He felt something rising inside him, as if he were a new human being. 'Mrs Florence I think I can do this,' he said, and for the first time since he had met her, he smiled properly.

'Good,' she said. 'It's the key to living a happy life. Now go home and think of something you want to ask for.'

As Jim left the house he stared at the bright orange sports car for a while and a short laugh of glee escaped him. It was an amazing sight. A miracle! So excited was he that he largely ran the whole way home and he felt as if the whole world was on his side – the birds singing in the trees, the horses in the field – everything was working with him. It was a feeling he had never had before. When he got home he greeted his mum with a big kiss on the cheek, which came as something of a surprise, but a big smile came across her face and a little of Jim's happiness spread from him to her.

'What time is tea Mum?' he asked, taking off his shoes in the hallway.

'About six o'clock,' she called from the kitchen.

'Great, thanks Mum,' he said, rushing upstairs to his bedroom.

Jim threw his bag on his bedroom floor, shut his door and sat on his bed. Then he wondered what to ask for. I could ask for a million pounds maybe, but how do I show active faith that I'm going to receive the money, he thought. That one seemed a bit tricky somehow. He could ask for a pet dog; he had always wanted one, but Mum and Dad had said they didn't have enough room. That one seemed a bit tricky too. Yes, he could ask for one and the Universe would provide him with one, but then where would they put it? Would the dog just become very sad with only a small garden to run around? Jim wouldn't want that to happen.

So what could he ask for? Maybe he could try the sports car again, and just do the exact same things that Mrs Florence did. But then he realised that the drive of his house was already clear and he had no bus pass to tear up.

Jim went to bed strangely disappointed that night. The happy glow inside had disappeared. He had left Mrs Florence with so much hope that he could have anything he wanted, but now that he was at home, he couldn't figure out how to get any of it. Every time he thought of something, he came up with some reason not to ask for it. Little doubts and fears seemed to creep into his mind. He decided to go to speak with Mrs Florence again the next day and ask for her advice.

Chapter Five

'So what did you wish for?' Mrs Florence said the next day. Jim had run straight down Black Hill and up to her front door after school. He hadn't even worried about Greg and his gang or whether his brother was still walking home with his new girlfriend. The orange sports car still sat on her drive.

'Well, I didn't in the end,' Jim said in response to her question. 'Every time I thought of something to get, something else got in my way.' He held his cup of tea and munched on a custard cream.

'What do you mean?'

Jim told her about how he had wanted to get a dog, but decided not to ask because they didn't have enough space at home.

'There's your problem,' said Mrs Florence when Jim had finished. 'You are full of doubts and fears. You are a worrier Jim. You think of something you want and then you think of a million different reasons why you can't have it. The Universe won't work for you if you don't work for yourself. You have to *believe* the Universe will give you what you want and you have to *trust* that it will sort everything out for you.'

'Right, ok,' said Jim. 'So should I ask for a dog then?'

Mrs Florence smiled. She always smiled and her smile always said that she knew something Jim did not know. 'Go home,' she said, 'and see what comes to you. Then when you decide what it is you want, rather than think of some ridiculous reason why you can't have that thing, think of something to show the Universe that you are ready for that thing, that you are expecting it to be provided. Do you understand?'

'Yes, I think so,' Jim nodded. 'Thanks Mrs Florence.'

When he arrived home, John was, surprisingly, already there. He was sat in an armchair in the living room, watching a cartoon on the television.

'Alright John,' said Jim.

'Yeah, I'm alright,' John said in reply, but he seemed more quiet than usual.

'You're home early.'

'Yeah, well, me and Michelle broke up.' There was a silence in the living room; Jim didn't know what to say. He had come home so enthusiastically after seeing Mrs Florence and now his smile was beginning to fade. He tried to figure out the best facial expression to show. Eventually he said 'Ahh, sorry.' A further silence followed. His brother gave a small nod of acknowledgement and Jim, feeling somewhat awkward, decided to leave the room.

When he got to his bedroom he had an idea. He could ask for something to cheer his brother up. He walked quietly into his brother's room, hoping to find some inspiration. There, on his bed, was a football magazine, perhaps a couple of weeks old, and when Jim opened it up it turned to an advertisement for a computer game: PremierFoot Soccer 5. This was it! Jim knew it for certain. John had always wanted PremierFoot Soccer 5. He had raved about how good it was after he had played it at a friend's house. There was a problem though. Jim and John did not own the right games console. So, thought Jim, I will ask for the game *and* the games console.

Jim peaked outside his brother's bedroom door. Nobody was around. He placed the magazine back on John's bed, open at the football game advertisement. He stood up and for some reason made sure that his shirt was tucked in. Then he said, 'Dear Universe, bring me a games console and a copy of PremierFoot Soccer 5. I give thanks that it appears now for me and my brother to use.'

And that was it. The games console did not magically appear, nor was there any flash of light or other special effect that you would expect to see in a movie of this kind. There was nothing. But Jim was not to be fooled. He knew now, having spoken with Mrs Florence, what he was to do next. He had to show the Universe that he believed it would provide him with the console.

He went back into his bedroom and opened his desk drawer. Underneath a pad of paper and a few magazines of his own was a birthday card from his aunty. Inside was a gift card for an online website.

'Happy birthday Jim. Buy something you want,' the card read.

Jim went downstairs and crept into the office. John was still sitting in a chair in the living room watching a cartoon. He paid no attention to Jim as he went into the office and turned on the computer. Jim went onto the website and searched for a controller for the games console he wanted. They were twenty five pounds each and Jim had thirty pounds on his gift card – perfect. He added the controller to his basket and ordered it using the gift card as payment. The order confirmation told Jim that it would take three to four working days to arrive, but Jim used the remaining five pounds to pay for express delivery. The controller would probably arrive tomorrow morning.

'What are you doing?' he heard his brother say from the living room.

'Oh, nothing,' said Jim, quickly exiting the web browser and turning the computer off. 'Just doing some research for homework.'

'Fair enough.'

Jim sat back in the chair with a big smile on his face. He had followed Mrs Florence's instructions exactly and he had shown active faith that the Universe was going to provide him with what he had asked. Not only that, he felt strangely happy that he had done something that wasn't just for himself but for his brother. Now he just had to wait.

He walked into the living room and decided he would continue to show the Universe that he expected his request to be carried out. Down by the television was a huge pile of DVDs that had been left there for ages. There was a space for them on the bookcase of course, but nobody had bothered putting them away. In his mind, Jim felt this was the perfect place for their new games console, so he began picking up the DVDs and putting them back on the shelf.

'What are you doing now?' asked his brother, slightly annoyed by the disturbance.

'Oh, nothing, just doing a bit of tidying up.'

'Fair enough.'

Jim placed all of the DVDs on the bookshelf then turned around to see an empty space next to the television. It was perfect for the games console. How could the Universe refuse him now?

Dinner time came round (shepherd's pie) and for some reason Dad was late. 'Where could your father have got to?' Mum asked Jim and John. Jim just shook his head and John just looked down at his plate, playing with his food, pushing the mashed potato up and down with his fork. They had decided to eat anyway and Mum put Dad's shepherd's pie in the oven to keep it warm.

About an hour later, Dad walked in. 'Where have you been?' asked Mum in an accusatory tone. But Dad had a big smile on his face. 'What are you smiling for?'

'Come into the living room and I'll show you.' He was carrying a couple of big bags. Jim and John were sat on the sofa watching something on the television.

'Right then,' said Dad, turning off the television with the remote control. 'The boss has been really pleased with how business has been going recently, and he said that he was particularly pleased with the work that I have been doing.' Everyone looked at Dad expectantly.

'Yeah,' said John. 'So?'

'So... he gave me a bonus!'

'Wow, Dad, that's amazing!' said Jim, genuinely very pleased for his father. Even John looked up with a more cheerful expression on his face.

'So, on the way home, I thought I would celebrate. Boys, I got this for your mum,' he handed her a box, grinning from ear to ear. Mum opened it up.

'What is it Mum?' asked Jim.

'Oh it's lovely!' she said, tearing up. She held the box for Jim to see. It was a silver necklace with a beautiful purple gem hanging from the middle.

'And... I got this for you lads.' Dad reached into another bag and pulled out a huge box. Jim couldn't believe it: it was the games console he had asked for!

'Oh Dad, that's amazing!' said John, a completely changed character from the one he had been earlier that day. Jim was speechless. Obviously he had asked for it, he had bought the controller for it, and cleared a space by the television, but he still couldn't quite believe that the console was now here, in his living room.

'Of course,' said Dad, 'it's no good just having the console, you've got to have a game to play on it as well, don't you?' And he pulled out from his bag a computer game.

'Oh wow Dad,' said John 'PremierFoot Soccer 5! This is brilliant! Thanks Dad!'

'That's alright boy, you're welcome,' said Dad. 'Jim, what do you reckon?'

Jim suddenly became aware that he hadn't said anything at all. 'I think it's incredible,' said Jim. 'Thanks very much. I think it will go perfectly just here.' He pointed to the spot next to the television where he had cleared a space earlier on.

'Yeah, that looks like a good place,' said Mum.

'Only one problem,' said John, unpacking the games console from its box.

'What's that John?'

'It's only got one controller.'

'Oh well,' said Jim. 'I don't mind taking it in turns. I'm sure we can get a controller for it soon.' And Jim, for the first time in a long time, felt incredibly happy. He didn't mind having to take turns with John to play the game because he felt he had something far greater than a games console. Mrs Florence had taught him something that he could use for the rest of his life. He would never have to worry about anything again.

John set the games console up and they spent the evening playing PremierFoot Soccer 5 while Mum and Dad watched. Dad ate his shepherd's pie and Mum wore her necklace and the whole family seemed to be enjoying themselves. Thank you, thought Jim, thank you so much. He wasn't sure who he was saying thank you to, maybe it was Mrs Florence, maybe it was the Universe, but he knew that he had to say thank you to somebody and so he did.

When he went to bed that night he felt that he should say thank you properly. He sat in his bedroom and, though it was dark, the room was lit by a half moon that was shining brightly through his window. He could hear his dad finishing off his night time routine in the bathroom; Mum and John had already gone to bed. There was a flush of the toilet and a running of water as Dad washed his hands and then went to his bedroom. When he was sure that he heard no one else moving around, Jim opened his window. He felt it was right to do it with his window open, though he wasn't sure why.

'Dear Universe,' he said. 'Thank you for the games console today. I am very grateful. Thank you also for making everyone so happy tonight. John was really sad about breaking up with his girlfriend and Mum and Dad are always arguing. Tonight was the first time in ages that we have all been really happy. So, as I say, thanks very much.'

Jim waited for a moment, but of course nothing happened. Then he shut his bedroom window, pulled his curtains and got into bed. He lay with his head on his pillow and a massive smile on his face.

Chapter Six

After school the next day Jim was desperate to go to Mrs Florence's house again and tell her what had happened. John, however, no longer together with his girlfriend, wanted to walk back with Jim. John made it seem that he was doing Jim a favour, but Jim knew better. Really he was the one keeping his brother company.

They stood outside school, just by the playground and the front gates. 'What are we waiting for?' asked Jim.

'Nothing,' said his brother.

Oh, right,' said Jim, after a pause. 'So, can we go then?'

'Not yet,' was his brother's reply. He leaned against the fence, trying to look really casual. He looked everywhere but at Jim.

'Oh… ok,' said Jim. He had known his brother in these funny moods before and felt it was best not to ask. It was one of the frustrating things about being a younger brother. Somehow John had a hold over him that meant that Jim would do whatever he was asked by John, no matter how annoying it was. Because the thing was, Jim really liked John. He really looked up to him, and these occasions where he got to spend time with his older brother were very rare.

Eventually Jim realised what, or rather who, they were waiting for. Coming out of the school gates on the other side of the playground was the girl that John had been going out with for the last week or so. She wasn't alone, however. Walking next to her, in the place that John used to be, was another boy, taller, with blonde hair.

John stared at them as they walked out, but the girl paid no attention, as if she were ignoring him. After they were out of sight, John said 'right, let's go,' picking up his bag and stomping off in a grump. Jim followed closely behind.

They went down Black Hill at some pace. As they came out of the alley, Jim spied Mrs Florence standing in her doorway. He was conflicted. He wanted to say hello, but also wasn't sure what his brother would think. In the end, the decision was made for him, for Mrs Florence raised her hand and gave Jim a wave and a smile. Jim shyly waved back.

'What are you waving at that crazy old witch for?' said John when they were some distance away.

'Er... she's my friend,' Jim replied.

'Your friend? How is she your friend?' said John, a bit too aggressively. Jim was fairly sure his anger was not really because of Mrs Florence, but behaved subordinately anyway.

'It's just... she says hello when I walk past after school and stuff.' Jim tried to sound as vague as possible. He wasn't sure why he didn't just tell John all about her. After all, she was the reason they could now play PremierFoot Soccer 5, but for some reason he thought that John would probably ridicule him.

'Well, if you want my advice Jim, you'll stay away. Kids shouldn't be mixing with adults like that.'

There the conversation ended and Jim began to get concerned. What if he had to walk home with John every day now and wouldn't be able to have a conversation with Mrs Florence again?

There was something else that bothered him as well. Something else that made Jim less keen to tell John all about her: the bright orange sports car was no longer sitting on her drive. In fact, it was nowhere to be seen. If it had been there it might have been a good way in to a conversation with John about everything she had taught him, but it wasn't. Jim couldn't help wondering where it had gone.

At home, a parcel was waiting in the porch. It was Jim's controller.

'Wow, where did that come from?' John asked. Jim explained that he had ordered it with his gift card. 'Blimey Jim, that was quick. You must have got express delivery.'

'Yeah, I did,' Jim replied, not wanting to reveal any more.

'Well, that's great. Now we can play two player on PremierFoot Soccer 5. That'll be so much more fun.'

That was pretty much Jim and John's evening. Mum made them sausage and mash with peas and gravy (one of John's favourite dishes). Dad had come home early; he had still got some money left from the bonus that his boss had given him, so he decided to take Mum out for dinner. Jim was surprised. He couldn't actually remember the last time that Mum and Dad had gone out for dinner without him and John. Mum got dressed up; she wore the necklace that Dad had given her the night before. Dad wore a shirt and tie, but not ones that he wore for work. Jim could tell that they were a lot happier than usual, which got him wondering whether actually the only thing they ever really argued about (and indeed the only thing they ever worried about) was money.

With Mum and Dad out for the entire evening, Jim and John had the run of the whole house, which meant PremierFoot Soccer 5 on the big telly in the living room all night and a massive bowl of crisps on the floor. John was much more cheerful than earlier on in the day. He was clearly not thinking about Michelle anymore and was keen to share with Jim his secret tips for scoring a goal or tackling an opponent. He even suggested getting some of his friends to come round for a competition, and Jim could play too, of course.

Jim was pleased to see that his brother was happier and, more than that, he was really excited about being involved in a competition with John's friends. He always thought they were a lot cooler than he was, so any contact with them was brilliant. The thing was, Jim didn't even like the game that much (he wasn't a huge fan of football), but he enjoyed spending time with his brother.

Their parents came home just after ten; Jim and John had been playing on the games console non-stop. Mum swiftly sent them both to bed, much to the relief of Jim's eyes, which were beginning to glaze over.

When he got to his bedroom, after he had brushed his teeth and put his pyjamas on, Jim felt a strange desire to talk to the Universe again. This bonus that his dad had received had made everything in the house seem a lot brighter, and he felt like he wanted to say thank you again. He opened his curtains like the night before, and opened his window as well. The moon was still high over Atlee Crescent, the road on which he lived.

'Dear Universe,' he began. 'I just wanted to say thank you again for the games console and the money that my dad got. It has made us all really happy over the last couple of days and I would really like that happiness to continue.' He paused. Then he realised there was something he wanted to ask for. 'Make it possible for me to see Mrs Florence again tomorrow so that I can talk to her some more about you. I give thanks for the conversations I will have with Mrs Florence tomorrow and afterwards.'

Jim waited, which seemed like the right thing to do, even though he knew nothing would happen, and then he closed the window, drew his curtains and went to bed.

Chapter Seven

'I've got cricket club after school,' said John in the car the next morning. 'So I won't be able to walk home with you. Is that alright?'

'Er, yeah, I guess so,' replied Jim, feigning disappointment. Secretly he was incredibly pleased. He didn't bother to remind John that he had been walking home without him for the first week of school anyway.

'Because you can wait for me if you want and then we can walk together.'

'No, I should be alright. It's not that far.' Since John had broken up with Michelle he had suddenly become a lot more protective over Jim.

'Fair enough.'

Dad was dropping them off at school as usual. He was incredibly cheerful this morning, even singing along to the songs on the radio, and Jim put it down to the meal he had had with Mum the night before. It was great to see them both in a happy mood, rather than arguing with each other all the time.

The school day dragged by. The novelty of going to a bigger place with different teachers and rooms for different subjects had worn off and, now that Jim knew roughly what to expect from most teachers, he wasn't too worried about them either. He didn't have maths with Mrs Numbers that day, who was the only teacher he was scared of, and Greg was off ill, so the main fears of Jim's school day did not exist. Jim was just a bit bored.

The end of the school day came far too slowly. It was a bright mid-September afternoon where the weather tried to prove that it still had plenty of summer left in it yet. When the bell went, Jim rushed out of the school gates, down Black Hill and straight to see Mrs Florence. He did not heed any of John's words of warning from the day before because he knew that John didn't know what he was talking about.

He ran straight up to the front door and knocked enthusiastically. The bright orange sports car was still conspicuously absent from the drive. Jim could hear Mrs Florence shuffling around behind the door. 'Hold on a minute my darling,' she said, her thick Cornish accent coming through the wood.

'Hello my darling,' she said as she opened the door.

'Hi,' said Jim, a big smile on his face.

'Have you come round for a cup of tea?'

'Yes please, if that's ok?'

'Of course it is ok. Come on in and make yourself at home.'

Jim took off his shoes in the hallway, then went and sat in his usual seat by the window. As always, there was a pot of tea and two cups ready on the table, as well as a plate of custard creams.

'So,' Mrs Florence said, pouring the tea. 'What did you ask for?'

Jim told her the whole story. He explained how his brother had been sad about breaking up with his girlfriend, about how he had seen the advert in the magazine and how he was inspired to ask for the games console, partly for himself but also to cheer up his brother. He told her about buying the controller with his gift card to show that he had active faith in the Universe, and about clearing a space by the television. Most significantly, he told her about how happy everyone was, how unusually happy, and how pleased he was about it too.

'That's brilliant Jim, well done. You've taken your first step into a happier and more interesting life.'

A big grin came across Jim's face because somehow he knew that it was true. Then he said 'but I don't know what to ask for next.'

'It's not always about asking for things. And anyway, did you know to ask for a games console?'

'No.'

'Well there you are then. Trust in the Universe and you will be inspired to ask for the things you want or need. That games console was the perfect thing to ask for at the perfect time. And what made that request even better was that it wasn't really for you, it was for someone else. You did it to make your brother happy.'

'Yeah,' Jim said and they were silent for a little while. Strangely, Jim didn't feel awkward, even though he might have done a week ago. Now he felt quite comfortable. As he sat there in the peace and quiet, an idea came into his head.

'Mrs Florence,' he asked, 'where has your sports car gone?'

'I sold it.'

'You sold it? Why?'

'Well, I didn't need it. A silly old woman like me doesn't need a bright orange sports car,' and she laughed as if she had just cracked a brilliant joke. 'I gave the money to charity.'

'But what about your bus pass? You tore it up.'

'It's alright, I've ordered a new one.'

'But, does that mean I have to sell the games console?' There was a strange logic to Jim's question, though he wasn't quite sure what it was. Mrs Florence laughed again.

'Oh no, of course not. You keep the games console until you feel like it is the right time to get rid of it.'

'Ok,' said Jim, nodding. 'So,' he asked after a moment, 'if you didn't need the sports car, why did you ask for it?'

'Because,' she responded, 'I wanted to show you something.' Jim waited. 'I wanted to show you what you can do if you trust in the Universe. That anything – *anything* – is possible if you ask and trust. People today Jim, they don't believe in magic or some kind of divine power because they aren't willing to believe in it, to trust that everything can and will be provided for them. But then, it is a hard thing to do. We humans, with our big brains, we find it very hard to let go.'

'I think I'm starting to understand that now,' said Jim. They both sat in silence for a few moments and for a little while Jim wondered what his parents and brother would think if they knew he was here, engaged in this conversation with Mrs Florence. They would probably tell him it was all a load of nonsense.

'There's something I don't understand,' said Jim. 'I guess it's linked to the sports car too. I don't mean to be rude Mrs Florence, but why... why do you live like this?' He paused for a moment and then felt he needed to expand his ideas further. 'I mean, you proved to me that you can get anything you want – *anything*, like you say. But you live here all by yourself in this little house, on the path home for a load of annoying school kids, in a small, boring town in the middle of the countryside. You could live anywhere, be and do anything, so why here?'

Mrs Florence looked at Jim. She had an amazing quality of expressing meaning through her eyes. In a way, Jim felt she was smiling through them. He had not offended her, he knew that. 'When you learn that you can have anything you want any time you want, you suddenly realise you don't want anything at all.' Jim looked at her quizzically. 'That might not make sense just yet. I've lived an exciting life Jim, been to some amazing places, but the Universe has put me here, and I trust this is where I need to be right now. I actually like this little town.'

Jim nodded. 'Thanks,' he said, because he knew he had asked a personal question that Mrs Florence didn't have to answer.

'And by the way,' said Mrs Florence in fake indignation, 'who says I live here all by myself?'

'Well, I...' Jim stuttered. 'I just assumed that...'

'What's my name Jim?'

'Mrs Florence.'

'There you are then.'

'You're married?'

'Well of course I'm married! Why do you think I call myself missus?'

'Er... I don't know. I just sort of assumed that... oh, I don't know.' Jim went red with embarrassment. It had not entered his mind that Mrs Florence was married. Whenever he called, she always seemed to be the only one in the house.

'That's alright, I'm only teasing you,' said Mrs Florence.

Jim sat listening. Suddenly he wondered if there was somebody else in the house right now; he couldn't hear anyone moving around in another room. And if they were here, why not just come and introduce yourself? A strange pang of suspicion came over Jim.

'You're wondering where my husband is, aren't you? And why you never see him when you call?' said Mrs Florence, as if reading Jim's mind.

'Er... yeah,' said Jim.

'Well, as you know you call round after school, about 3:30. My husband happens to be at work at that time. He doesn't get back until about 5:30.'

'Ahh, I see. What does he do?'

'He's a florist. A very good one too. Such beautiful expression he shows in his arrangements, don't you think?' And she gestured to the bouquets around the room.

Jim let out a sound of understanding. The flowers had been such a glorious addition to her room every time he had visited and now he knew why. Part of him wanted to go to the local florist in the high street to see Mrs Florence's husband, but he knew he was just being nosey.

'Sometimes,' said Mrs Florence 'I can just stare at these flowers for minutes at a time and just get completely lost in them.'

Jim smiled and nodded politely, for, much like some of the comments Mrs Florence made earlier, this was one that he respected but didn't really understand. How could you get lost in flowers just by staring at them?

'Mrs Florence, I'm sorry to ask the same kind of question again,' Jim began. 'But why does your husband go to work? He doesn't need the money, does he?'

'Perhaps you can ask him yourself one day?' She said, and smiled. 'Gosh, is that the time?' A clock in the hallway chimed to signal that it was four o'clock.

'I'm really sorry Mrs Florence,' said Jim, jumping up. 'I didn't realise what the time was. I'd better get home quick otherwise my mum will start to panic.'

'That's ok Jim. Always a pleasure. Come by any time.'

Jim grabbed his school bag and shot out of the front door, waving goodbye to Mrs Florence as he ran down the road.

Chapter Eight

Jim knew that he wasn't a popular boy. He knew that none of the girls fancied him and he knew that he wasn't funny or confident or very good at sports. He told himself that he wasn't that bothered: when he looked at those boys that were considered popular, he often thought that they were foolish. They seemed to get the attention of girls by being rude to the teacher, or nasty to another boy or just plain being stupid. Despite this, Jim was bothered. He wanted girls to like him and he had hoped this might change when he got into high school, somewhere down the line.

In the meantime, Jim made himself feel proud through his academic ability. In primary school his test scores were fairly high; he was often in the top five in class for results and this was because he knew he could do the tests if he put his mind to them. His parents had told him repeatedly that he should work hard in school so that he could 'get a good job' and occasionally Mum would warn him not to 'end up like your father', who did not achieve any secondary qualifications. Because Jim was a worrier, these things obviously concerned him, so he put a lot of effort into doing well; he wanted to make his parents happy and he wanted to get a good job later in life.

At the start of secondary school, he felt as if he was doing quite well in most lessons. He kept up with what was taught in class and was able to answer most questions that the teacher asked. In one subject, however, this was not the case. His new maths teacher, Mrs Numbers, absolutely terrified him, and with that terror came failure. He found in some cases he was getting calculations wrong that he was sure he knew how to do in primary school. His confidence dropped and he became more and more panicked in her lessons. If you asked Jim to explain why Mrs Numbers scared him though, he wouldn't have been able to tell you.

It was with great fear, then, that Jim came home the next day with the knowledge that they would have a test in maths on Monday of the next week. He wasn't able to speak with Mrs Florence about it, though he would have liked to, because John had insisted on walking home with him again, and John had already made his feelings about her perfectly clear. Jim did not want to be seen to be ignoring John's advice. He looked up to him too much.

'You alright Jim? You look a bit worried,' said John on their way home.

'Ahh, yeah, just found out we have a maths test on Monday.'

'Oh, that's nothing to worry about,' replied John. 'They give it to all of the year sevens in September. It's so they can figure out what set to put you in.'

Jim gulped. The test wasn't just any test, it would determine which set Jim went into for the rest of the school year, maybe for the rest of his time there. He didn't want to be stuck in the bottom set with all the naughty kids. 'Oh right,' he said, trying to sound relaxed.

'You know everything you need to know already Jim. It's everything they taught you in primary school. No problem for you, you've always done really well in your maths.'

'Yeah,' said Jim quietly, and then quickly changed the subject to whether they were going to play any PremierFoot Soccer 5 that evening.

The maths test continued to bother Jim into the night. For some reason he wasn't any good at maths anymore; he just knew it. Mrs Numbers had given them a revision sheet that showed all of the key skills they needed to demonstrate in the test, but whenever Jim looked at it his head began to swim. It didn't seem to make any sense to him at all.

He distracted himself for the rest of the evening by playing PremierFoot Soccer 5 with his brother, and then, as he was getting ready for bed, he had an idea. He knew that he could ask the Universe to give him things; perhaps he could ask the Universe to help him out in the test as well. Just like before he drew back his curtains and opened his window to the night. He quite liked the habit of doing the same things every time he spoke with the Universe. Then, when he was certain that everyone else had gone to bed, he began.

'Dear Universe, make me successful in my maths test on Monday. I give thanks for the good grades I receive in maths.'

He waited, as always, knowing nothing would happen, then he closed his window and pulled back his curtains. He sat in the dark for some time. Now I need to think of some way of showing faith that the Universe will work for me, he thought. He looked around the room and eventually his eyes landed on the revision sheet that was sitting on his desk. He stared at it for a moment then decided he knew the answer. He scrunched it up and threw it into his bin. There, he thought, I know the Universe will work this out for me so I don't need to revise. Jim climbed into bed and went to sleep, satisfied that he no longer needed to worry about the test.

Saturday came and, despite his confidence of the night before, Jim couldn't help thinking, every now and again, that he should be revising for his maths test. Little things, like when his brother mentioned the revision sheet in the middle of a game of PremierFoot Soccer 5, kept bringing his mind back to it, and so he couldn't help thinking that perhaps he should revise. Jim felt, however, that to do so would not be showing faith and trust in the Universe, and he knew how important that was.

On Sunday he had a bit of a surprise. John had organised the PremierFoot Soccer competition with his mates. They played downstairs in the living room. Jim got knocked out in the third round, though he was quite pleased that he had managed to get that far. One of John's friends, Stan, was particularly annoying and kept going on about how good he was, but Jim managed to beat him 2-1. This was not the surprise. The surprise was that, when Jim went up to his bedroom after being knocked out, he found his maths test revision sheet, unscrunched and sitting on his desk.

'What the –' He picked it up and looked at it in disbelief. He had definitely thrown it away; how could it have brought itself back to his desk? He wondered if, since it was now here, he should spend some time looking at it, but he convinced himself that he should stick to not doing any revision, and so threw the sheet of paper in the bin.

'Oh Jim,' said Mum at dinner that evening. 'I found your revision sheet in the bin yesterday so I put it back on your desk. Hope that's ok, I was worried it might have fallen in there by mistake.'

'Oh ok, thanks Mum,' Jim replied. He decided it was best not to explain either way.

On Monday Jim felt reasonably relaxed until he got to school. He and some of the boys in his maths class were standing around in the playground and they began to discuss the test. All of them, it seemed, had decided to do some revision for the test.

The morning flew by and before Jim knew it he was standing outside the maths classroom for the afternoon lesson. They had to line up in silence outside the classroom door, standing up straight rather than slouching on the wall. Mrs Numbers would come out and stare at them for a few minutes and then, silently, signal for them to enter. When Jim walked into the room he saw that it had been reorganised. Tables and chairs had been moved apart in such a way that nobody could copy off anyone else. In front of each seat was a booklet – the test – that each pupil needed to complete.

'Now then,' said Mrs Numbers when everyone had sat down. 'This is a test. You should not talk to anyone or look at anyone else's paper. You will have forty five minutes to complete the test and then we will mark them together as a class. Any questions?' Nobody put their hand up. 'Then you may begin.'

Jim opened the first page. He looked at the question. It was something to do with fractions. He had felt quite confident with fractions in primary school. But now, for some reason, they seemed confusing. He scribbled away for about five minutes, then eventually he got an answer that he thought might be right. Jim checked how many more questions he had to answer – nineteen! – with only forty minutes left! He tried to stay confident because he knew the Universe would be helping him out, but the panic was rising nonetheless.

Jim was about halfway through the test paper when Mrs Numbers told the class that they needed to stop writing. He was in complete despair and sat in silent horror as she handed everybody a green pen and told the class that she would be showing them the answers and they would need to mark the papers themselves.

Mrs Numbers projected an image of each of the questions on the board and she talked the class through them one by one. At the end of the lesson, Jim had worked out that, of the half of the paper that he had completed, he had managed to answer about half of that right. Mrs Numbers said that, as a final task, the pupils should work out their percentage. Jim, who suddenly seemed very good with percentages, calculated that he had scored a dismal 27%.

'Well class,' said Mrs Numbers. 'I would normally ask you to call out your scores so that I can complete my mark sheet, but the bell is about to go, so put up your chairs and leave your test papers on my desk as you make your way out.'

Jim breathed a sigh of relief. The thought of having to share with the rest of the class that he had only achieved 27% was too much for him to consider. As the bell went, however, and they got outside the door, Jim overheard the others discussing how they had got on.

'I got 86%,' he heard Tom saying to someone behind him. This made Jim's score even worse; in primary school the two boys had been fairly equal in maths scores. In fact they had a friendly competitiveness. He moved swiftly through the crowd before Tom caught up with him and asked how he had got on.

'I got 45%,' he then heard Greg saying. This was unbelievable. Even Greg - stupid idiot Greg, he found himself thinking – had got a better score than him. Even Greg!

This was too much for Jim. Too much on two levels: he was disappointed that he had performed so poorly in the test, that he had been beaten by so many others, but he was also disappointed that he had put his trust in the Universe and it had not delivered as he had asked. He suddenly felt himself becoming very angry at everything and left school quickly, without even bothering to wait for his brother as he was supposed to. He wanted to see Mrs Florence and let her know how angry he was. He started to think that perhaps this whole Universe business was a big fat lie, that it was a lucky coincidence that his dad had come home with the games console, that Mrs Florence had just rented the sports car for a day. She just wanted to have a bit of fun with him, a laugh at his expense.

He ran down Black Hill and knocked furiously on Mrs Florence's door. He had not realised as he did so that tears were flowing down his cheeks.

'Why Jim, whatever is the matter?' she asked as she opened the door.

'You lied to me!' he said. He was surprised at how angry he was.

Mrs Florence did not respond with anger, nor deny the accusation. Instead she answered with one questioning word: 'Jim?' And it seemed as if, for the first time since Jim had known her, there was more than just that happy emotion pouring from her face. It was clear that she was in some way hurt. It wasn't as though she was offended though, it was something else, as if she was hurt that he was hurt.

They simply looked at each for a few moments, he heaving and sobbing with rage, she with the questioning, hurt silence.

Eventually she said 'come in,' left the door open and went to sit in the living room. Jim stood on the doorstep for a few moments before deciding to go inside.

'What's wrong, Jim?' Mrs Florence said, pouring the tea.

'I don't want any tea,' said Jim rudely. Mrs Florence looked up, gave Jim a kindly look, looked back down and poured two cups anyway. She leant back in her chair with her own cup in hand and waited. Her slow, deliberate breaths were a stark contrast to Jim's emotional heaving.

Finally Jim broke the silence. 'Your whole blinking Universe thing is a lie!'

'Is it?' Mrs Florence replied calmly. 'Why?'

There was something about Mrs Florence's manner that was beginning to break through Jim's aggression. His next response was more annoyed than angry. 'I got 27% in a maths test today.'

'Ahh,' Mrs Florence responded sympathetically. 'I see. And you asked the Universe to get you a good grade?'

'Yeah,' said Jim, now more miserable than annoyed. 'I was worried about it. I've been doing really badly in maths lessons lately. I used to be so much better in primary school. So I did everything I was supposed to. I asked the Universe in the right way, and I showed active faith, but today I didn't even get through half the paper. Even that stupid idiot Greg did better than me!'

'Who's Greg?'

'The boy that tried to beat me up,' he grumbled.

'Ahh ok.' Mrs Florence took a sip from her cup. 'Tell me how you showed active faith.'

'I didn't revise. I threw the revision sheet into the bin and played computer games all weekend.'

'I see.' Mrs Florence put down her cup of tea, rested her elbows on the arms of her chair and clasped her hands together in front of her face. She leant her head onto her hands and pursed her lips as if she were thinking. 'Most of the time Jim, if you want something from the Universe, you have to show you are working with it – going in the same direction if you like.' She paused for a moment to let this sink in. 'So, when you want to show active faith, that demonstration should be something that helps you to get that thing. It's got to be something positive. For example, if I was playing football and I asked the Universe for me to score a goal in my next game, it would be unhelpful for me to sit at home and not practise for the entire time before the match, even though it might seem as if I am showing active faith by not appearing worried. It would be more positive for me to practise shooting regularly beforehand, and then, during the game, my demonstration of active faith would be to make sure I was in the penalty box a lot with the confidence that the Universe would provide me with a ball to score with. Does that make sense?'

Jim thought that it probably did make sense, though he was partly baffled by the idea of Mrs Florence playing football on a Sunday morning.

'It is like when you got your games console. The things you did to show active faith were incredibly positive. That's why it worked.' She reached forward and picked up her cup of tea again. 'Let me ask you something,' she said, sipping from her cup. 'Did you feel like you wanted to revise throughout the weekend even though you threw the sheet away?'

'Yes,' said Jim. He was beginning to feel himself being swayed back to Mrs Florence's way of thinking.

'You should have trusted your instincts Jim,' said Mrs Florence. 'When you bought that games controller, when you cleared that space by the television – these were all ideas that just came to you, weren't they?' Jim nodded. 'That is your *intuition* Jim, you must trust it. It is the Universe giving you hints of what to do next.'

'Ok,' said Jim, nodding his head some more. He knew what he needed to do next, whether it was from the Universe or not. 'I'm sorry for the way that I behaved a few moments ago.'

Mrs Florence made a hand gesture, a sort of waving away, to suggest that it didn't matter.

'No, really,' said Jim. 'It was very rude of me.'

'I accept your apology,' she said, smiling.

'I should get going,' he said, picking up his school bag and heading to the door. 'Thanks for the tea and… everything.'

'No problem,' said Mrs Florence. 'There's one more thing though Jim,' she said, following him to the door. 'The Universe, it only ever wants you to be happy, to be satisfied. Sometimes we look at an event in our lives and we believe it to be a failure. We think about it in such bad ways and we lose faith. But often our failures are successes in disguise, and if we begin to think about them in that way, then we find ourselves on a continual path of happiness.' She smiled again. She always smiled. Here was a woman who always viewed her failures as successes. 'Have a safe journey home.'

Jim's expression was one of deep thought, of searching for meaning and understanding. 'Thanks,' he said, 'hopefully see you again soon.'

On his walk home he pondered the idea further. It certainly seemed a radical idea to view all of your failures as successes, almost nonsensical, but then a lot of what Mrs Florence had told him in the time he had known her would seem nonsensical to most of the people that he knew. He imagined telling his mum to view a burnt dinner as a success, and what her angry response might be. He couldn't help smiling at the idea.

But maybe he could view it as a success. After all, if he hadn't done so badly on the test he wouldn't have gone to speak to Mrs Florence, and what he learnt there was far more important than how he did on some silly year seven maths paper. He felt as if he knew some magical secret that no one else had the faintest idea about. He thought about how all of the other kids at school always ridiculed Mrs Florence, but she had taught him such incredible things that they would never know.

He walked in his front door with a big smile on his face.

'Alright bro,' John said as he walked in. 'Where have you been?'

'Sorry John,' he said. 'I just went round a friend's house after school.' He thought John might ask more questions, but he didn't.

'Fair enough,' he said. 'Fancy a game of PremierFoot Soccer?'

'Of course!'

The next day Jim went into school feeling as if the maths test was a success. It might not have been a high grade, but in terms of his life, it was an important achievement. He wasn't afraid to tell people he only got 27%, and even laughed it off when Greg tried to tease him.

At registration, something amazing happened. Mrs Numbers came in and asked to speak to Jim outside. When he got outside the form room, Mrs Numbers said 'Hi Jim, how are you this morning?'

'Yeah, ok thanks Miss.'

'Good. I just wanted to have a chat with you about your maths test yesterday.' Mrs Numbers said that she was a bit worried with Jim's test result as it didn't really reflect the kinds of grades he was getting in primary school. Was everything ok? She asked. Was there anything she could do?

Jim was astounded. He stuttered some response about being really nervous and not feeling that comfortable in class.

'I understand,' said Mrs Numbers, smiling. 'Listen, I'm going to assume this test was just a bit of a blip, ok? I'm going to ask the head of maths to put you in a set that would be appropriate for your primary school maths results because that's where I think you should be. Ok?'

Jim could not believe it. Mrs Numbers was being nice. Maybe he had completely misjudged her after all. The way she was talking to him, it seemed as if she genuinely cared about him and how he was feeling.

'Er, yeah,' said Jim, 'that's great.'

'That would mean that you would be in my set though Jim. Would that be ok?'

'Yes, definitely.' In the length of an instant his opinion of Mrs Numbers had completely changed. It was obvious to him now that he wouldn't want any other maths teacher than her.

'Great. See you next lesson,' she said and walked off down the corridor.

Jim couldn't help standing outside the classroom for a little bit longer. He wanted to make sure the huge grin was no longer on his face before he went back inside. The Universe had sorted everything for him. By viewing the test as a success, it really became one. He was no longer scared of Mrs

Numbers, he knew that he would be in a good set and he had learnt so much more from Mrs Florence. Jim was amazed. It was a miracle.

Chapter Nine

John had not seemed his usual self. The initial excitement of getting the games console had masked the fact that he was unhappy for a while, but not for long. John still played PremierFoot Soccer 5 of course, he loved it, but it wasn't enough to keep him completely contented.

Jim noticed that John was often grumpy. This was normal in the way that John behaved with his parents; his interactions with them were often short and grunt-like. With Jim, however, John was normally quite courteous, for an older brother. Recently, though, things had changed. He had been snappy, aggressive, and often wanting to spend time alone. It was during the following weekend, when a few of John's mates had piled round for another PremierFoot competition that Jim started to understand why.

Initially, John was not willing to let Jim play, but his friends convinced him otherwise. 'We need another player,' said David, one of John's closest friends. 'Besides, Jim's pretty handy at PremFoot. I like to have a bit of a challenge.'

'Alright,' grumbled John, and went out to get some drinks. It was while he was out of the room that David gave Jim a bit more of an insight into John's current mood.

'Bit grumpy at the moment, isn't he Jim?'

'I'll say.' Even if Jim did not think that John was grumpy, he would have probably agreed with David because he liked him.

'It's all because of Michelle, you know.'

Jim liked this conversation about girlfriends. He felt quite mature to be let in on it. 'I thought they broke up ages ago.'

'Yeah, two weeks,' said David. 'Then she started going out with Michael James in year ten. John was annoyed – as you would imagine. He fancied Michelle all last year, finally got the courage up to ask her out at the start of this year and pretty much as soon as she became unavailable, Michael James steps in and asks her out. She can't resist an older boy, so she dumps John and starts going out with him instead.'

'I see.'

'Yeah, but if that was all, it might not be that bad. The trouble is that she keeps bothering John, texting him and saying she still wants to be his friend, or telling him how annoying Michael James is being. Your brother doesn't know whether he is coming or going.'

At this point John came back into the room with the drinks and they began to organise the competition. It was a round robin – everyone would play everyone else – and they would run it like a league. The person with the most wins at the end of the afternoon would be the winner of the league. Jim was happy with that. It meant that he would get to play quite a few games throughout the afternoon rather than just one or two and then get told to go to his bedroom.

John was midway through his game against Jim when he got a text message from Michelle. He was so focused on playing that he didn't notice his phone light up. Stan, however, did notice, and quickly grabbed the phone.

'Got a text message from Michelle, John!' He said, with an annoying grin across his face. John didn't say anything, but just continued to play the game, a scowl growing across his face.

'Don't be an idiot, Stan,' said David.

'Shall I tell you what it says?' Stan persisted.

'Dave, can you get my phone off him please?' John said. David pounced on Stan, who quickly relinquished the phone.

'Alright, alright,' he said. 'I was only messing around.'

'Well don't,' said David. 'You know how he feels about stuff to do with Michelle.'

'Sorry John,' Stan said.

In all of this, Jim had noticed John was not playing as well. There were a couple of times when Jim could have scored easily but decided not to. He didn't want to put his brother in an even worse mood.

Throughout the rest of the afternoon John continued to be subdued. The competition ended, the boys went home and John went up to his bedroom, he said to do some homework. Jim couldn't help thinking about what Mrs Florence had said about viewing failures as successes, and he wanted to share this with his brother, he just wasn't sure how. He knew that if he just told John straight out he would tell him to get lost, to stop talking rubbish and go away, but he wanted to help his brother.

He went to his bedroom and muttered a request to the Universe. 'Dear Universe, thank you for helping me to share with John the stuff about failures and successes and for John to understand what I mean. I give thanks that you show me how I can do this in the best way.' Mrs Florence had told him about the importance of asking for things to be done in 'the best way.' Otherwise, she said, you might end up getting what you want but at the expense of losing something else, or someone getting hurt.

Then Jim sat there. He decided that he wasn't in a rush to speak to his brother and that the Universe would provide him with the right opportunity to sort things out. He looked at his desk and thought that he might use this time to do a bit of homework, just like his brother was. He didn't have any that needed to be in for Monday, so really he was getting ahead of himself for the rest of the week. This could only be a good thing.

He completed the work fairly quickly. In the end it only took him ten minutes, and Jim felt he deserved a reward so went downstairs to get himself a snack from the fridge. He pulled out a chocolate bar, and, spotting a second one behind it, decided to take it for John. He walked back upstairs and knocked on the door.

'What?' he heard John say abruptly through the door.

'I just,' said Jim, opening the door a little bit, 'brought you a chocolate bar to help with your homework.' John was sat at his desk with a science textbook in front of him. He looked at Jim and for a moment it wasn't clear whether he was going to be grumpy or friendly.

In the end he said 'cheers bruv,' and held out a hand to receive the chocolate bar.

'How's the science homework going?' Jim asked as he handed it over.

'Oh, yeah, it's alright,' said John, sighing. 'It would be better if Michelle would just stop texting me.'

'Why don't you ask her to?' asked Jim, but he got no reply. John just looked at him as if he were stupid. Jim knew the answer anyway; it was because John still fancied Michelle and secretly hoped that they would get back together. Then he suddenly felt brave as some words came into his head. 'It seems like a really good thing that you split up with her.'

'Go away Jim,' said John, a look of disdain on his face.

Jim felt that it was right not to push. 'Ok,' he said, and walked back to his bedroom. No sooner had he sat down at his desk when his brother came storming in.

'Why exactly is it a good thing that I've split up with Michelle?' he demanded.

'Well, it's just she seems like she's messing everyone around. She goes out with you one minute and then starts going out with Michael James, but she's still texting you. She'll probably dump Michael soon and start going out with someone else.' John looked at him but said nothing. 'I'd just tell her to stop texting you and then forget about her, safe in the knowledge that it was a good thing she dumped you so quickly instead of messing you around for ages.'

John frowned; perhaps it was a frown of annoyance, perhaps it was a frown of confusion. Jim wasn't sure. He couldn't tell which, and no words from John, who had been fairly quiet through most of the conversation anyway, could enlighten him, for he turned around and walked back to his bedroom.

Once upon a time, Jim would have panicked at this reaction. He would have been dreadfully worried that he had upset his brother and that John would be annoyed with him. Now, however, he didn't mind. He felt strangely calm. He knew that the Universe had helped him out and he had said the right words at the right time. He decided to leave his brother alone and went to help out his dad, who was working on a car in the garage.

After school on Monday John and Jim walked home together in the rain. They hadn't spoken much on Sunday evening, other than a quick exchange of the words required to start a game or two of PremierFoot Soccer, but Jim felt there was no issue between them and decided to wait for him at the school gates anyway.

In the past Jim might have complained about the rain, been grumpy about the fact that he had to walk home and get wet, but today, as with so much in his life, he decided to apply Mrs Florence's philosophy. He decided to consider the rain a success. And indeed it was. It had been a long hot summer, with very few rainy days. According to Jim's dad, there had been a hose pipe ban, though he wasn't really sure what that meant. This rain would be a welcome drink for all of the plants and wild animals. Not only that, because Jim wasn't annoyed at the rain, he actually quite enjoyed the sensation of all of his clothes getting wet through to his skin. He found it amusing.

John and Jim squelched down Black Hill and towards Mrs Florence's house. Jim wondered if Mrs Florence would be there waiting and had already decided that he didn't care what John thought, he would wave to her and say hello if she was. He might even go in for a cup of tea and invite John too if Mrs Florence didn't mind. In the end, she wasn't there, so they walked on by without incident.

When they were some way past Mrs Florence's house, walking down the hill that ran next to a paddock that led to their road, John started speaking. 'I took your advice about Michelle,' he said, looking straight ahead at the road.

'Oh yeah?' said Jim, trying to sound casual.

'It was good advice. You were right. She is just messing me around. It is a good thing that we split up. I told her to stop texting me and she has, and I feel a lot happier now.' He smiled. 'Cheers Jim.'

'That's alright,' said Jim, this time trying not to sound so smug.

'How did you get to be so wise anyway?'

'Dunno. Must just be the people I hang out with.'

John laughed. 'Yeah, right. Anyway, we did some group work in Geography today and because I wasn't moping over Michelle I got chatting to this girl called Jennifer.'

'Oh yeah?'

'Yeah,' said John, and laughed. 'We're going to meet in town on Saturday.'

'Nice one,' said Jim, smiling, and they squelched their way home.

Chapter Ten

It seemed that the romance between John and Jennifer blossomed quickly. So much so that by October John was going round Jennifer's house for dinner an awful lot and Jim was free to walk home by himself, stopping in on Mrs Florence whenever she was available. While he enjoyed spending time with his brother, this was an arrangement that he was most happy with. He still got to see John a fair amount, but he also got to see Mrs Florence and spend lots of time practising PremierFoot Soccer without his brother being there. He was particularly pleased that he had mastered the skill of the direct free kick and was able to score from most places within ten yards of the box. The next time one of his brother's competitions came round, he knew that he would be top of the league.

Jim felt happy, happier than he ever thought he would in high school. All of the things that he thought he was worried about just seemed to dissipate. He found himself regularly asking things of the Universe in his head throughout the school day, little things like having a good lesson or enjoying a game of football at lunch (even though he never thought he was very good at sports) and as a result everything seemed to fall into place. He even found that his issue with Greg seemed to completely disappear. He wasn't sure what it was that did it. Somewhere along the line he had started to use Mrs Florence's idea of viewing everything to do with Greg as a success, and suddenly he stopped feeling nervous around him. In a way he decided to see Greg as a friend rather than an enemy and so Greg just left him alone. In fact it was better than that; sometimes they played football together, even on the same team, and at others Jim had walked right past Greg and his brother on Black Hill and all that happened was an exchange of a friendly greeting.

After school he would continue to visit Mrs Florence and drink tea and eat custard creams. She would listen to him talk about all the things that had happened throughout his day, how he had viewed this as a success, how he had asked the Universe for that, and then how the Universe had worked things out perfectly for him. Mrs Florence would listen and smile, but not once did she seem surprised. One day Jim was telling her about how things had changed between him and Greg.

'And just now,' he said, munching on his custard cream, 'I walked right past him going down Black Hill and he said "Nice save today, Jim," – because I was in goal at lunchtime.'

'That's brilliant, Jim,' said Mrs Florence. 'You're not scared of him anymore. When you were scared of him you attracted the bully inside of him, but as soon as you stop fearing him and had faith that the Universe would sort things out for you, the bully inside him ran away. Faith not fear, Jim, faith not fear. That's the key.'

'Yeah,' said Jim, and then, wanting to share his own idea about how things had worked out. 'It was sort of like viewing things with Greg as a success.'

'Exactly, by doing that you had faith. Faith in the Universe inside of him.'

More and more Jim felt that he was beginning to understand Mrs Florence's ideas, but this one was lost on him.

'I don't understand,' he said. 'The Universe inside of him?'

'Yes, Jim. Have you ever wondered what I mean when I say the Universe?' This was an interesting question. Jim had never specifically considered that idea. When he thought about the Universe he thought about space, an infinite space, filled with stars, somewhere up there, maybe. But he also knew that idea didn't really work out as the same thing that Mrs Florence was talking about.

'Is it space and stuff?' Jim attempted, rather uncertainly.

'I guess you could say that it is space and stuff. But it's more than that too,' Her face became more expressive and her hands more animated. 'The Universe is everything,' she said, and her hands swept around her in a huge globe. 'It *is* space and stuff, but it is also these chairs, these flowers, these custard creams, your teachers, your friends, even

Greg. It. Is. All. One.' And as she said each word her two hands came closer and closer until they were held together in a clasp. 'And when we ask it for things, we do it because it wants us to. It wants us to work with it because it is an essential part of our being. *The* essential part of our being. That's why so many people are unhappy Jim! They think they are all alone, that they have to graft for every penny that they have, that they might lose it all at any moment. When the truth is the Universe will give it all to them if they only believed that it would. The truth is that nothing is truly lost because we are all one.'

Jim took a deep drink from his cup of tea while he processed what she had just said. 'It's a strange idea, Mrs Florence,' he replied. 'And I have to tell you that if you had told me a few weeks ago that I was one with Greg Mitchell I'm not sure that I would have believed you. But today, I don't know, it feels oddly correct, like you've just reminded me of something that I completely forgot. It's weird. It feels like your words are ringing a bell inside me.' Jim was trying to describe the feeling in his stomach. It felt like the day that Dad walked in with the games console in a plastic bag. It felt like joy. He couldn't think of anything to say for a while, but he also felt like that was ok. He looked at Mrs Florence and she looked at him and they both smiled that knowing smile. Before, Jim had always felt like he was on the ignorant side of that knowing smile, but today was different. Today he felt as if he completely understood.

If someone had come into the room at this moment and interrupted they might have understood what was happening, but probably not. There were no bright lights, no amazing noises, no phenomenal occurrences, only Jim and Mrs Florence smiling. But even so, Jim knew. Jim felt that what was happening was pure magic. Inside.

'Do you see, Jim?' Mrs Florence asked, almost in a whisper.

'Yes,' said Jim. 'I do see.'

'One day,' said Mrs Florence. 'Everyone will see.'

Jim imagined this future world of everyone getting along. It was funny: he could have imagined all the nations of the globe coming together and shaking hands, having fun and singing in harmony; he could have imagined them dismantling all of their weapons and recycling them into farm machinery; he could have imagined them all getting together and playing a massive competition of PremierFoot Soccer 5, but he didn't; he simply imagined the world that he knew. For him this really meant one thing, sitting at home with his family at dinner time, perhaps eating a roast dinner. They were talking, who knows what about, and then John and Jim laughed at something Dad said, then Mum and Dad laughed too, then Dad reached out for Mum's hand and she smiled at him. It was beautiful and he felt a tear roll down his cheek.

Jim's attention returned to the room. He looked at Mrs Florence. 'How?' he asked. 'How will everyone see?'

Mrs Florence looked at him, her eyes searching his. 'I don't know,' she said. 'Maybe, slowly and surely, there will be more people like you and me, and we can spread the word. But honestly Jim, I don't know.'

'Ok,' he said. The clock in the hallway chimed to say that it was four o'clock. Jim gave his thanks for the tea and custard creams as always, said he would probably be back again the next day and then shot off home as quickly as he could.

Chapter Eleven

All the way home, all the way through dinner and all the way through the evening, Jim couldn't get Mrs Florence's words of that afternoon out of his mind. 'One day,' she had said, 'Everyone will see.' And Jim's mind had flown off into his own perfect world where his family sat around the dinner table and were happy.

He compared it to the actual dinner he had that evening. Before they started eating, Mum was bashing around in the kitchen, slamming down saucepans far harder than was needed, while also being immensely grumpy when either he or John offered to help. Then during dinner, neither Mum nor Dad really spoke to each other at all. There was no laughter and no holding hands. Then, after dinner, Mum and Dad descended into an argument over nothing in particular. Mum told (rather than asked) Dad to wash up. Dad responded by shouting back that she shouldn't speak to him like that, Mum responded in kind and the argument grew and grew and grew until eventually Dad went upstairs to their bedroom to watch television. It was funny in a way; they were like a couple of teenagers.

It wasn't funny to Jim though, nor John. He got up, shut the living room door and said 'I wish those two would shut up.'

Jim responded with a 'yeah, me too.' Because, for the most part, that was all Jim and John had wanted – peace and quiet. They would have much preferred that Mum and Dad were out and the place was calm than anything else. Until this afternoon. Jim hadn't realised, until Mrs Florence had said, that really what Jim wanted was not for his parents to simply be absent, but for them to be together and to be happy.

The truth was that the arguments had been going on for so long that it wasn't really clear where they all began. It was like some old blood feud between two gangster families. It went back so many years it seemed impossible to unpick where things had started to go wrong. The brief happiness that appeared to blossom between Mum and Dad after he came home with his bonus was only temporary. Within a matter of a week or so they were back to bickering and snapping at each other whenever they could.

A typical evening went like this: Mum would get home from work and start preparing dinner. There would doubtless be a couple of other household jobs she would try to achieve at the same time. Dad would get home about half an hour later, entering through the back door and attempting to squeeze past Mum while she was preparing dinner. Argument number one would begin here. Argument two would take place at the dinner table, when Mum would scroll through a list of things she wanted Dad to do, argument three when Dad either didn't do the tasks or did them with varying degrees of failure. It was always a disaster, but no matter how Jim looked at it, he couldn't see a solution.

Jim looked at the situation and felt he understood both sides of the story. Mum and Dad both had to work, but then Mum was often the one who had to do all the housework and cooking and so on as well. But then when anyone did the housework they either got it wrong or got in the way, so that Mum would have a go at them and they would realise it was easier not to bother helping out. Then Mum would get even more annoyed and round they would go in a big circle. Dad could get really angry, aggressive sometimes. It was very upsetting when Jim was younger.

'Are we the kids in this family, or are they?' said John.

'Yeah,' said Jim. Deep down, as much as he tried to understand how his parents were feeling, he just wanted them to stop arguing for the sake of their sons. It was as if they were completely blind to the pain they were causing.

So that night, after everyone else had gone to bed, Jim sat on his bed in his pyjamas, curtains open and the window open too, and he thought about what to do. He didn't want this situation; he wanted the one that he had imagined in Mrs Florence's house. He wanted that brief happiness that his parents had felt when Dad came home with the extra money to last forever. Could he ask the Universe for that? Or perhaps he should ask for a big lump sum of money? He had thought that might be the issue. If they had enough money they wouldn't have to work, and if they didn't have to work they wouldn't be so tired and so maybe they wouldn't argue. But then there was the question of how much he should ask for; would a million pounds be enough? And how on Earth would he show active faith for receiving a million pounds?

Would it be easier to simply ask the Universe for his parents to stop arguing? Or to view the marriage as a success? It was so difficult to see a way forward, and Jim didn't feel inspired to come up with a solution like in the other situations the Universe had helped him with. In fact, he didn't feel confident at all. The more he thought about it, the more he felt like he was bruised on the inside. There was only doubt and fear rattling around inside of him, fear that there was no solution to this problem and that his parents would just carry on this journey straight to disaster. How quickly his cheerfulness had disappeared!

That night he didn't feel he could ask the Universe to help with anything to do with his parents because he was convinced that nothing would work. In the end he resolved to lean his head out of the window and say 'Dear Universe, I give thanks that these feelings of doubt and fear disappear.' He laid down in bed and, so keen was his mind to forget the sadness, he fell asleep almost immediately.

The next day he woke up in a grumpy mood. The feelings from yesterday had yet to disappear. In fact it felt as if they were spreading. He did not feel happy to go to school and he didn't feel confident that the Universe would resolve all of his problems for him. He ended up not asking for anything all day, and, as a result, had the worst day he had had at high school so far. Suddenly everything – not just his parents' marriage – looked as if it was going to go wrong: he got told off for talking in English, even though it wasn't him; he had a surprise test in science and he thought he had done really badly on that; he got pushed over during football at lunch. He even got into an argument with Tom during some paired work in art. Everything was falling apart.

He was keen to see Mrs Florence as quickly as he could. John was going round to Jennifer's house for dinner, so he was free to visit her without worrying about his brother's judgements. When he arrived at her house, however, and he knocked on the front door, there was no answer. Oh no, he thought, now everything really is going wrong. I'm having a terrible day and Mrs Florence isn't even here to help me.

He sat on the front step, head in hands, angry with the world. He started picking away at some loose stones around his feet and then threw them into the road ahead of him. He wasn't sure how long he sat there – perhaps only ten minutes – before he decided to give up and go home. Just as he was walking away, however, he saw Mrs Florence coming up the road from the other direction.

In one hand she carried a plastic bag of shopping and in the other she held her walking stick and used it to support herself. Jim had never seen Mrs Florence moving more than the few steps between the front door and the living room; this was something of a surprise to him. He was so used to seeing the energy in her face – the aliveness in her expression – that to see her hobble up the road was a bit alarming. Mrs Florence was really old. She spied Jim just outside her house and raised the hand carrying the plastic bag as a wave. Jim waved back and wondered whether he should go to meet her or whether he should just wait. In the end he decided to stay where he was.

'Ahh Jim,' said Mrs Florence, panting heavily as she came towards him. 'It's lovely to see you. I just had to go out and pick up some more custard creams. Come on in.' She unlocked the door, spent a moment or two fiddling with her shoes and then sat with a thump into her chair. She continued to breathe heavily.

'I can make the tea today, if that's easier Mrs Florence?' said Jim.

'That would be wonderful, thank you Jim.' She gave him directions to the kitchen. 'It should all be laid out and ready for you.' And indeed it was. There was already the teapot with two teabags inside it resting on a tray; next to that were the two cups. Jim spotted the kettle, already filled with water, and turned that on to boil. He took the milk from the fridge and waited.

As he stood there, he spied a photograph on the shelf above the sink. It sat in a plain wooden frame. There was a family inside, a mother, father and two children, a golden retriever too. They were at a beach somewhere. It was a beautiful sunny day so they all had sunglasses on, but Jim could make out Mrs Florence's face. He wondered how long ago this was. She looked so much younger. Her hair was brown rather than grey, and her face still had that energy to it. He looked at the children and could see echoes of Mrs Florence in their faces, the classic echoes of being a close relative. These must be her children. And next to her, Mr Florence, the florist. Jim felt a pang of something. He had spent so much time telling Mrs Florence about his life that he had forgotten to ask about hers.

The kettle boiled, Jim poured the tea and took the tray into the living room. He set it down on the table as normal and then sat in the chair he always sat in.

'That's it, good lad,' Mrs Florence said, still breathing deeply, but not as heavily as before. 'Let's leave it to brew for a minute. Phew. I am getting old.' It was the first time Jim had ever heard her say anything that didn't seem entirely positive about life.

'Could you,' said Jim, 'ask the Universe to stop you getting older?' Jim felt embarrassed asking the question. For one thing, it felt silly; for another, Jim knew, following a stern word from his aunty one

Christmas, that it was rude to talk about a woman's age.

Mrs Florence simply laughed. 'Yes, I guess I could.' She laughed even harder when an idea popped into her head: 'I could ask the Universe for a beautiful young body again and show active faith by going out and buying a load of those bikinis!' She continued to chuckle to herself, then became more serious. 'These days I tend to only ask the Universe for one thing.'

'What's that?'

'That I follow its plan.'

'How do you mean?' asked Jim. Once again he felt as if he were entering some new territory of understanding that he hadn't known before.

'The Universe – just pour me a cup of tea please my darling – the Universe has a plan for us all. It is what we are meant to do while we are here. The thing is, because it is what we are meant to do, it tends to be the thing that will make us most happy when we do it. So nowadays, when I wake up in the morning, I simply say "Dear Universe, let me follow your plan for me this day." And that's it. I'm not sure,' she said, beginning to laugh again, 'that the Universe wants me to be younger again, though if I find a bikini lying around today then I'll take that as a hint!'

Jim laughed too and tried desperately not to think of Mrs Florence in a bikini.

'I er,' began Jim, not sure whether it would seem like prying to ask, 'saw a photo of your family in the kitchen.'

'Ahh yes,' said Mrs Florence and smiled. 'Can you go and get the picture so that I can look at it?' Jim went out and brought it back. 'Hmmm. It was beautiful, Dunwich, probably about thirty years ago. I think Becky – that's Becky there.' She stopped to point out her daughter. 'Would have been about twelve and Steven would have been about ten. That's one of my favourite photographs of all of us together.'

'I didn't realise that you had children,' said Jim.

'Oh yes,' she said. 'And grandchildren.'

'Really?'

'Yes, Becky has two, Elizabeth and Sarah, both teenagers now. I have a picture of them here somewhere.' She reached down to a photograph album that rested by the side of her chair. She opened it up and turned to a picture of her with two young girls sitting on either knee. In a similar way to the photograph in the kitchen, it was a sunny day and the sea rolled calmly in the background.

'Do you get to see them much?'

'I saw them last year. They live over in New Zealand now. Becky married a nice man called Alex who is from Auckland. He was working over here in London when they met and fell in love. They moved out there when the girls were just toddlers.'

Jim browsed through the photographs. 'Have you ever thought of moving out there with them?'

Mrs Florence smiled. 'Well, we did for a time. We only moved back here in the last twelve months. The Universe called us home.'

Jim wasn't sure whether he could ask her to be more specific. For some reason he felt that maybe he shouldn't. Instead he decided to ask something else. 'And what about your son, Steven?'

'He is why the Universe called us home.' Again Jim wanted to ask what that meant, but felt as if he shouldn't. In the end, he didn't have to, because Mrs Florence answered his unasked question. 'He suffered from drug addiction Jim. At one point he became very low and took an overdose. When Mr Florence and I found out we flew straight home. He was finally willing to let us help and care for him then. Steven stays in a rehabilitation centre not far from here. I get the bus to see him every morning.'

'I'm sorry,' said Jim.

'What for?'

'For asking. It must have been very upsetting.'

'Never apologise for asking questions Jim. And don't pity me either. I have had, and continue to have, a wonderful life. Steven is mending now and we are closer than we ever were.'

Jim looked down into his lap. His doubts and fears about his parents started to come back at this story of Steven, and they grew.

After a moment, Mrs Florence, who had been quietly watching him, spoke. 'What's the matter Jim?'

'I'm just upset. I know that you say things are getting better now, but that is a sad story. You are one of the most amazing people I have ever met, and the things you have taught me about the Universe make me think that absolutely anything is possible. They make me think I can do anything and that I will be happy for the rest of my life. But I don't understand how you can know this stuff and be able to ask for whatever you want and yet your son still suffered in this way. My parents…' And Jim, surprising himself, began to tear up at this point. 'My parents always argue with each other. They are hardly ever happy. I wanted to ask the Universe for help, but I couldn't think of what to ask for. I hoped that I could come and speak to you today and you would have a solution, but now I'm not so sure. I mean, if you can't stop your own son from suffering, what hope do I have of helping my parents?'

The tears at this point were in full flow. They flooded down his red cheeks like waterfalls. Mrs Florence was standing next to his chair – she had stood herself up – and was holding her arms out to him. When he looked up at her, he saw that she too had tears in her eyes. He flew into her arms and cried, deep, deep cries. They didn't speak, but just held each other for a while.

When it seemed that Jim's tears were coming to an end, Mrs Florence let him go and reached for a box of tissues, passing them to him before taking one herself and sitting back down. Jim sat down too and wiped his eyes. It felt like an incredible relief to cry about his parents. He hadn't realised how upset he was. Even though the situation hadn't changed, he felt in some way better.

'That has been building up in you for some time my darling,' Mrs Florence said. 'You have just had a powerful healing.'

'I do feel a bit better actually,' said Jim, sniffing.

'It is important to talk about these things Jim, otherwise they build up. They clog you up emotionally and mentally. You wanted the Universe to give you some help about your parents, and it has.'

'Ok, I feel a bit better,' said Jim, still sniffing slightly. 'But what good is it if my parents are still unhappy. What good is it if they are still suffering?'

'Oh Jim, my darling. You are a lovely, thoughtful boy, aren't you? See how much you care for your family. The thing is, there is only so much that you can ask the Universe to help other people. I want you to remember what I am about to tell you now. It is going to sound like I'm being nasty, and selfish, but I'm not, ok?'

'Ok.'

'Everyone is responsible for their own happiness. You have a personal, one-to-one relationship with the Universe. The active faith that you show it is the bridge, the telephone that connects you to it. Your faith allows your prayers to be heard. Because you believe the Universe will give you what you need, it does.

'Not everyone feels the same way. Ultimately, it has to be their choice to believe or not believe. You could go home and tell your family, but they might not believe you. They have to have faith and you can't give it to them. They have to do it for themselves.'

'But when they are suffering?'

'Your parents have created that themselves. They have enough money but they always worry that they won't have enough. So your dad is in a job that he doesn't really like, having to drive so much further than he wants to, and your mum does a job that she would enjoy if she didn't do so many hours. They are so scared of not having enough that they work too hard and that puts them in a bad mood. And because of that they have forgotten to love each other. They do love each other, you know, it's just buried under all the other stuff.'

Jim was baffled by how Mrs Florence knew all of this stuff. As she described the situation, he felt that she had defined the problem perfectly. Yes, his parents did just worry about money and work too hard as a result.

'So why can't I just ask the Universe for some money and then give it to them? It made them happy for a little while before.'

'Because it will only change their situation, it won't change them. They'll still feel the same way about money, still worry they don't have enough. Still argue with each other.' Jim wasn't sure about this, but accepted it anyway.

'Is there nothing I can do then?'

'There is one thing you can do. The most important thing. You can love them. Don't judge them, don't resent them, just love them. And always view your relationship with each of them as a success. Love can do wonderful things for making people see things differently. It might just take some time.'

Mrs Florence passed Jim a custard cream and he munched on it pensively. The clock in the hallway had chimed four o'clock some time ago, but Jim had been so caught up in the conversation they were having that he hadn't realised.

'One thing I'm wondering about,' he said.

'Go on.'

'Well, if everyone is responsible for their own happiness, and they have to be the ones to have faith to get out of whatever they are in, does that mean that I shouldn't bother ever helping anyone?'

'Jim, you know, you have the answers to the questions you ask already, inside of you. Remember the Universe within. I could answer for you, but I want you to try to answer for yourself. Close your eyes. Take slow, deep breaths through your nose, in and out of your belly. Now, I want you to ask the question again in your head, and then just breathe. Wait for the Universe to provide you with the inspiration of an answer.'

Jim sat there. His hands rested in his lap and he breathed in and out. He felt the slow, steady rise and fall of his stomach, could feel the air flowing in and out of his nostrils, could hear it like the faint rolling of the ocean. The sweet scents of Mr Florence's flowers that adorned the room filled his nose and calmed his mind. After a few minutes he opened his eyes. Mrs Florence, who had also been sitting with her eyes closed, opened hers a moment later.

'Well?'

'Well, I think you should always try to help people if you can, but respect them if they don't want you to.'

Mrs Florence smiled at him.

'Is that the right answer?' He asked, uncertainly.

'It is the right answer, for you, at this moment in time. Which, by the way, is probably about time you went home.'

Jim looked at the clock. It was half past four. 'Oh gosh, I'm sorry Mrs Florence, I had no idea. Thanks very much for today. I've gotta go!' And he rushed out of the door and ran all the way home.

Thankfully, when he got there, he was the first one back. John was at Jennifer's house, and Mum and Dad were both still at work, so he didn't have to explain his whereabouts. He did find a note from Mum, however, asking Jim to turn the oven on at a quarter to five. He looked at the clock: 4:44 pm. Phew, he thought. That was perfect timing.

After he turned the oven on, he thought some more about what Mrs Florence had said. Love them, she had said. And when Jim thought about it, he had been getting so annoyed with the arguments, that he hadn't always been as nice to them as he could have been, nor as helpful around the house. So he looked around and thought of the chores that he could do. He laid the table, vacuumed the living room and even washed up that morning's breakfast things. He didn't resent it, instead he was happy to do it because he knew it was a small sign that he loved his mum.

When Mum got home, it was clear she was grateful that Jim had done the few things that he had, and the effect of this was amazing. After doing a couple of other things for dinner, Mum sat down in the living room with a cup of coffee. 'Ohh,' she said, relaxing. 'It's nice to get off my feet and have a break for a few minutes. Thanks for doing all that stuff when you got back Jim.'

'No problem Mum,' he said and smiled at her.

When Dad got home, he didn't have to squeeze through the kitchen while Mum was trying to prepare dinner because all of that was done already; Mum was sitting down in the living room relaxing. At dinner, the list of jobs that needed doing was depleted because Jim had helped out in advance. Mum, being in less of a bad mood, asked (rather than told) Dad if he would be able to have a look at her car because it didn't seem to be accelerating as it normally did.

Before Dad could reply, Jim said 'I'll give you a hand with that if you like, Dad.'

There was a brief look of pleasant surprise on Dad's face. 'Oh, alright boy. We'll have a look a bit later on, shall we?'

'Yeah.' And so the second argument was avoided. Jim had made the job of taking apart Mum's car far more bearable by offering to be there too.

Strangely, there was a silence at the dinner table. Normally the speech that took place was bickering between Mum and Dad, but because there was nothing to bicker about, neither of them had anything to say.

'How was your day today love?' Mum said to Jim. Jim smiled. What a lovely dinner time.

After dinner Dad and Jim sat down and watched an episode of Star Trek ('just while our dinner dies down,' Dad had said) and then they got outside and worked on Mum's car. Far from being a chore, Jim enjoyed it. He was in awe of his father, who seemed to know so much about how to fix a whole manner of things, and took a great deal of pride in the fact that he was considered by family, friends and neighbours alike to be a safe pair of hands. The thing was, because he often got so annoyed with his dad for arguing all of the time, he forgot how much he liked him. He was funny, and when he wasn't around Mum, he was often quite relaxed.

Jim went to bed that night feeling with absolute certainty that the evening had been a clear success. Mrs Florence, as always, had been completely right. All Jim had to do was to show love to his parents. It was all he could do. The next morning he overheard his parents arguing in the kitchen – it sounded like it was something to do with who had gotten into the bathroom first – but he didn't despair. He remembered what Mrs Florence had told him: everyone is responsible for their own happiness. Yes, he could show them love, but it wouldn't change them forever. Only they could do that. He wasn't going to beat himself up about it.

Chapter Twelve

It was coming towards the end of Jim's first half term at high school and, as he rode to school in the back of his dad's car, he reflected on how much had changed. Of all the things that he had been taught over those six or seven weeks, nothing compared to the sheer wonder of the things that Mrs Florence had shared with him. He felt as if the rest of his life would be one glorious adventure from now on, because the Universe would always provide for him when he needed it.

He thought about all that the Universe had helped him with since meeting Mrs Florence: the games console, Greg, his brother's relationship with Michelle, Mrs Numbers and the Maths set, finding a way of dealing with his parents, as well as lots of little day to day things. He was surprised at the list that he made. When he thought back to that first request – the sports car – he thought he would have asked for loads of expensive stuff, but that wasn't what he did at all. He somehow didn't feel the need for any of those things; he was happier having the Universe resolve his social issues for him.

School that day was much the same as usual and Jim chalked it up to being a success. John wasn't going to Jennifer's for dinner that evening, so Jim had to walk home with him. As before, he was convinced that, if Mrs Florence stood in the doorway, he would wave and say hello. He didn't care what John thought: Mrs Florence was his friend. When they got to the bottom of Black Hill, however, and exited the alleyway, the door to Mrs Florence's house was closed. Jim didn't worry, as this had happened a few times before, and continued on his way.

'Bruv,' he said to John.

'Yeah?'

'I was thinking about trying to help out around the house a bit more. You know, chores and stuff.'

'Oh yeah?'

'Yeah, just take the load off Mum and Dad a little bit.'

'Sounds like a good idea. They do have to work pretty hard.'

'Yeah, that's what I thought.'

There was a pause in the conversation and they continued to walk in silence. Then Jim said, 'everything alright with Jennifer?'

'Oh yeah, cheers bruv. She's great. We get on really well, you know.'

'That's good.'

In his head Jim thanked the Universe. Thank you for my family, he thought. Thank you for showing me how to help them.

It was a weird feeling for Jim. He was pleased that they were happier than they had been, and he knew that he had played some role in that, but even so he didn't feel like he could claim the credit for it, and nor did he want to.

When they got home Jim and John looked around the house and made a list of what needed doing. Jim got in the kitchen and prepared some vegetables for dinner; John got the washing off the line. Jim vacuumed the stairs and John laid the table. They couldn't think of anything else that needed doing so they sat down to play PremierFoot Soccer. Just as they sat down, Jim said 'oh, I know,' and popped up to put the kettle on to make a coffee for Mum when she got in.

Just like yesterday, the evening was pretty much argument-free and Mum didn't even have any jobs for Dad to do. Jim and John even suggested they didn't play on the games console so that Mum could watch some film she had been wanting to watch for weeks. It was set on an island and had lots of singing. It wasn't really something Jim was interested in, but they sat round as a family and watched it together anyway, which obviously pleased Mum a lot.

When Jim got to bed that night he couldn't think of anything to ask for, but once again he thanked the Universe. He thanked it for everything.

The next morning was Friday, and not just any Friday, but the last Friday before the half term break. Jim had enjoyed his first half term, it was true, but he was excited at the prospect of having an entire week of getting up whenever he wanted. He hadn't made any definite plans for the time off, though he and Tom thought they might meet up at some point. Otherwise he thought he would try his best to do some housework and play lots of PremierFoot Soccer with John (providing John wasn't out with Jennifer). He had thought that he might try to visit Mrs Florence as well, though he would have to find out when she was going to be in.

At school the lessons were fairly easy. The teachers refused to show films, much to the disappointment of the likes of Greg, but Jim didn't mind. He liked learning, and he wouldn't want to watch films in the lessons he had that day anyway: technology, science, PE and art. All of them were practical, interactive subjects. He could watch a film at home if he wanted.

In art they had been working with clay. The school had its own kiln and the teacher, Mr Ronald, had promised to have the designs all fired and glazed for that day's lesson so that the pupils could take them home. Jim had already decided that he would give his candleholder to Mrs Florence as a way of saying thank you for all that she had done.

It was an unusual design. Jim had taken inspiration from the sculpture of the figure sitting cross-legged that sat on a shelf in Mrs Florence's living room. The main body of the pot was the torso and the legs of the figure, then the head was the top, with the scalp missing. He had spent a long time on it, even coming in during lunchtime to add extra detail. When he had finished, he wondered if he might be able to turn it into a candleholder, so he carefully cut two holes, one in the front and one in the back of the torso, so that you could easily slot a tea light inside. When Mr Ronald handed it to him on that Friday afternoon, he couldn't have been more pleased.

'It's an excellent design Jim,' Mr Ronald said. 'I really like how you chose an Eastern culture to influence your work and the detail you included is superb. Well done.'

'Thanks sir.' Jim grinned from ear to ear. He had asked the Universe to help him produce the candleholder for Mrs Florence and now that he looked at it, he couldn't believe that his hands had moulded the clay. He wrapped it carefully in his school jumper and placed it on top of his books in his school bag. He couldn't wait to give it to Mrs Florence.

When the bell went, he walked quickly out of the school gates. He would have run but was concerned about damaging his candleholder. John had told him that morning that he would be going round Jennifer's house, so he did not have to hang around, but made a quick path towards Black Hill. Standing at the top, eating sweets out of a paper bag, was Greg, his brother and his brother's friend. Jim smiled.

'Alright Greg,' he said.

'Alright Jim,' Greg replied. And Jim strolled on by.

He bounded down Black Hill, turned the corner and came to the exit of the alleyway, but before he walked out and up to Mrs Florence's house, he stopped. He knelt down, opened his bag and unravelled his jumper. His work was still in one piece. It looked good.

He wrapped it back up in his jumper and returned it to his bag. Jim had thought carefully about how he would give it to her. He would sit down and have tea, as always, chat and eat a custard cream, and then, just before he was about to leave, he would hand it over. He smiled at the thought of the look on her face.

Jim walked up to Mrs Florence's house and knocked on the door. To begin with there was no response, then Jim heard some movement from inside. It was unfamiliar, however, not the normal shuffling of Mrs Florence's feet, and Jim began to feel that something was not quite right.

The door opened. Standing in the doorway, looking down at him was a man that Jim assumed to be Mr Florence. He recognised him from the photograph in the kitchen, though he was much younger then. There was something else too; his face seemed to have been touched by a sadness that wasn't there in the photograph.

He was about the same height as Mrs Florence, though in the picture Jim thought he looked taller. He was bald, with some grey hair round the sides, and he carried a thin, well-trimmed moustache above his upper lip. He wore a light green jumper, under which was a shirt, and a pair of light coloured trousers. Jim thought that Mr and Mrs Florence were about the same age, but to someone so young it was difficult to tell for sure. There was something strangely similar about his face, however, something reminiscent of his wife.

'You must be Jim,' he said, and he offered a weak smile and a hand. Jim hadn't shaken anyone's hand before, but reached out and felt a warm, firm grasp around his. 'Come on in,' he said.

It felt odd, as if he were entering the house for the first time. He thought about all of the times he had confidently walked in and out of that front door, but now he felt uncertain once again. He stood in the living room while Mr Florence sorted a few things on the table where the pot of tea normally sat.

'Have a seat,' he said. 'Would you like a cup of tea?'

'Er,' said Jim. 'Yes please.'

Mr Florence disappeared into the kitchen. Jim sat in the chair and looked around. On a table behind Mrs Florence's chair was a bouquet of flowers in a glass vase, a beautiful combination of different shades of pink. But elsewhere the room was bare. It was not the usual jungle of exotic colours and scents that Jim was so used to seeing when he came to visit. The room seemed dull, lifeless, without them.

Mr Florence entered carrying two mugs of tea. It was not the normal teapot and cups that Jim was familiar with. The mugs were bigger, less delicate. Jim's mug had intricate drawings of different New Zealand birds on them, their names written underneath: the tui, the kea, the kiwi. He liked the unusual spellings of the words and wondered how they were pronounced.

'Jim,' Mr Florence said. 'I have some bad news.' Jim's stomach dropped. He suddenly felt very cold and empty. He put down his mug of tea. 'Eva – Mrs Florence – passed away yesterday.' The cold and empty feeling remained. Jim was confused. How could she die?

'I don't understand.'

'She died, Jim, yesterday, very peacefully.' Mr Florence spoke incredibly gently, as if Jim were the one to lose a lifelong partner and not himself.

'How?' Jim's speech was quiet, weak, like nothing at all. He felt dizzy. He felt his eyes becoming blurred, his hearing fuzzy. From some distant place, he heard Mr Florence say 'Jim, are you alright?' and then he was gone.

Jim woke up. He looked up at an unfamiliar ceiling and a face. It was Mr Florence's face. He was lying on the floor in the living room, his head resting on a cushion.

'Jim,' he heard Mr Florence say. 'Can you hear me?'

Jim groaned.

'You're ok,' said Mr Florence. 'You just fainted.'

Gradually, Jim's memory came back to him. Mrs Florence. Dead.

'I'm sorry,' mumbled Jim, feeling how incredibly impolite it was to faint in someone's living room.

'Don't be sorry lad,' he said. 'It's perfectly alright.' Jim sat up. 'I'm afraid your tea has gone cold. Would you like another?'

'No, I'm fine, thank you.'

'It is a terrible shock, I know.'

'How did it happen?' Jim asked, delicately. He wasn't sure if he was asking too sensitive a question.

'Well, she died in her sleep Jim. She went to bed as normal, and then didn't wake up the next day. The doctor said it was natural causes.' He spoke quietly, carefully, but also calmly.

'I'm very sorry Mr Florence.'

Mr Florence nodded. 'We are both very old, Mrs Florence and I. We have had our time here I think. One of us had to go first.'

Jim had no idea what to say in reply. 'Is there anything I can do to help?'

Mr Florence thought about it for a moment. 'I have to organise the funeral. It would be useful to have someone else around for that. If you don't mind Jim, that would be very kind of you.'

'I would like to help,' said Jim. 'Shall I come tomorrow?'

'Yes please. I have to see our son in the afternoon. Would you be able to come in the morning?'

Jim said he could. 'I had better be going Mr Florence.'

'Ok, Jim.'

'See you tomorrow.'

Jim walked home, dazed and shocked. It didn't seem real to him, to be told that someone who was always there wasn't going to be there anymore. This was Jim's first experience of death and he had no idea what to do or think or feel. Any thought of the Universe was out of his mind; he was below thought.

When he got home, the house was empty. He walked straight upstairs and into his bedroom. And he lay down on his bed, looking up at his ceiling. He just continued to look. The dull emptiness continued to sit inside of him, waiting.

Outside he heard Mum's car pull up on the drive. He heard the engine go off and the door slam closed. He heard her walk into the house, through the kitchen, drop her bags down in the hallway. He heard her looking in the living room to see if he was there and he heard her call his name. He didn't respond. He heard her walk up the stairs and stand outside his door.

'Jim?' She said. 'Are you in there?'

'Yeah,' he said, dully.

'Can you...' Jim's mum began as she opened the door. Then she stopped when she saw Jim on the bed. 'What's the matter?'

And that was it. The dull emptiness erupted into a great explosion of grief. The bond between a mother and her son opened up something deep within Jim and he just let go. He suddenly felt young, so very young, and his mum came to him and put her arms around him.

Jim cried and she rubbed his back. 'What *is* the matter?' she said.

Jim wiped his tears. 'Mrs Florence died,' he said through his tears.

'Who?'

'Mrs Florence.'

'The wife of the florist? Who lives at the bottom of Black Hill?'

'Yeah.'

Jim's mum continued to rub his back. She watched him with concerned eyes. 'How do you know Mrs Florence?' She asked.

'She was my friend,' he said. Through his tears he told her how she had helped him get away from bullies one day after school and then invited him in for tea. He told her that he started going to see her most days after school, on the way home, that he would stop in and have a cup of tea and a custard cream. 'She helped me a lot mum,' he said. 'I talked to her about school and stuff and it made all those things a lot easier to cope with.'

Mum didn't say anything in response, but sat and rubbed his back. Jim could hear her slow, soothing breathing and he remembered how much he loved his mum.

'Ok darling,' she said. 'Ok.'

'Mr Florence needs my help getting stuff ready for the funeral. Is it alright if I go round tomorrow morning?'

Mum was going to protest – surely Mr Florence has other people to help, adults – but something inside stopped her. She saw how upset he was, how close he had become to this woman and she decided not to. Perhaps it would help him to come to terms with what had happened.

'Yes, of course you can darling,' she said. 'I'm going to start making dinner – fish pie, your favourite. Are you going to be alright?' Jim nodded. 'Ok, let me know if you need anything.'

Mum went downstairs and Jim continued to lie on the bed. He heard Dad come home. There was no argument in the kitchen; instead he heard them talking in quiet, respectful tones. Jim could just make out Mum telling Dad everything that had happened.

Dad came up the stairs, popped his head around Jim's bedroom door. 'Alright boy?' he said.

'Yeah, ta.'

'Ok,' he said and went to get changed.

That night Jim went to sleep immediately. Unlike most other nights for the last month or so, Jim did not speak to the Universe. He felt uncertain about it, maybe hurt, betrayed, that it had not kept his friend alive. But these feelings were all too muddy, and he did not look at them directly. He got into bed, closed his eyes and the stress and strain of such an emotional day carried him off to oblivion.

Chapter Thirteen

It was a bright October Saturday morning and Jim woke up at seven o'clock. It wasn't the fuzzy, gradual waking up of most mornings; it was immediate. He opened his eyes and there he was.

Mum, Dad and John were all still asleep, but Jim did not want to rest. He got up straight away, keen to do something. He slipped on some jeans, a t-shirt and a hoodie and snuck downstairs. He ran the cold water tap, filled up a glass of water and drank it all in one. He made himself a bowl of cereal and ate it standing there in the kitchen. He didn't want to sit in the living room and eat it in front of the television.

He left his bowl and glass in the sink, went back upstairs and splashed some water on his face. He brushed his teeth and went to the toilet. He went back into his bedroom and packed a small backpack. He put in a book (in case he had to wait around anywhere), a bottle of water, a waterproof jacket and the candleholder that he had made for Mrs Florence.

He checked his watch. It was only a quarter past seven. Perhaps it was too early to see Mr Florence on a Saturday morning, but he had to get out of the house. He crept back downstairs, left a note in the kitchen to say that he had already gone to help Mr Florence and went for a walk. He decided he could do a circular walk of the town and end up at Mr Florence's house for about half eight. If it was too early he could always just hang around.

Gildstow was a small market town, big enough to have a high school and a supermarket, but not big enough to have a train station. It was surrounded with open fields growing barley and rapeseed, and one could easily walk around the whole town in under an hour. Some of the buildings dated back to Tudor times, and the townspeople took great pride in the fact that its name featured in the Domesday book.

From his house, Jim walked down past the supermarket, round the edge of town where some new houses were being built. The development was built on an old ammunitions dump and his dad had told him the rumours of secret passages running all over Gildstow from that point. Archaeologists had also completed a series of digs in the area and discovered Roman coins and pottery.

Jim decided to skip the town high street and headed straight for the riverwalk. It ran all the way along the back of the town and Jim knew that he could take that path and only see the odd early morning dog walker. When he was younger, Jim's grandparents would bring him and John to feed the ducks, but he didn't think about that now.

Jim walked. He didn't stop, he didn't admire the scenery, he just walked. He felt that if he stopped he might have to think, and that was something that he didn't want to do. His outburst with his mother the day before had opened the gates of his sadness; he understood that Mrs Florence was dead, so he wasn't avoiding the feeling, he just didn't want to wallow in it. He thought he might be able to somehow burn it off if he just kept walking.

He walked up, out of town towards the abandoned pillbox, a relic from wartime. Its floor was littered with broken glass and beer cans now, not a place for boys to play at war. He walked down towards the war memorial, and up past the old primary school. He walked up to the start of where a railway station once stood and from there onto his high school.

Jim checked his watch again. It was only eight o'clock. It would only take him another five minutes to walk to Mr Florence's house, at most. Still, he felt drawn there anyway. If it was too early, he would wait.

He walked past his high school and thought how ridiculous it was that he was here on the first morning of the half term break. He started to walk more quickly, just in case anyone saw him and thought that he had forgotten he didn't have to go to school that day. Then he began his normal walk home, just round the corner and down Black Hill. As he walked down he began to feel sad. He knew that he would never walk down this hill to see Mrs

Florence again. He would never get to visit her after school again to talk through the happenings of his day. He would just have to walk straight home.

Jim sat down in the alleyway, unable to go further. A few tears formed in his eyes. He began to worry. He realised that he wasn't just crying for the loss of Mrs Florence, he was crying for the return of his life as it was, with all its problems and fears. The thought of going back to school for a second half term suddenly became terrifying. He buried his head in his arms.

'Jim?' Jim looked up. It was Mr Florence. He was carrying a small bag of shopping. 'Are you ok?'

'Ah, yeah,' Jim replied. 'I was just...' He scrambled to his feet and wiped his eyes with his sleeve. Mr Florence didn't wait for further explanation.

'Thanks for coming so early. Have you had breakfast?' He said, holding up his shopping bag. 'I picked up some things for bacon rolls if you fancy one?'

'Yes please, if that's ok.'

'Of course. Come on,' he put his hand on Jim's shoulder and smiled, then led the way into his house.

'I like my bacon crispy,' Mr Florence said as he placed four slices into the frying pan. 'How about you?'

'Yeah, the same, thanks.'

The heat brought the bacon to life. It hissed and sizzled, changed shape and colour almost instantly. The deep, salty smell filled the kitchen.

'I was thinking,' said Mr Florence. 'I sprung the news about Eva on you yesterday. I'm sorry about that.'

'That's alright,' said Jim. 'I don't think there is any easy way of doing it, is there?'

'No, I suppose not.'

Mr Florence buttered the two rolls. 'Tomato ketchup?' He asked.

'Yes please.'

'Good lad.'

The bacon was brown. It had shrunk and become crispy and hard. Mr Florence placed two slices in each roll and closed them. He handed one to Jim and then signalled for them to go and sit in the living room.

They sat down and ate the rolls in silence. Jim looked around the room he had studied so often before. He spotted the crucifix and he suddenly started to wonder.

'Mr Florence, where is the funeral going to be?'

'It's at the church, on Friday.'

Jim nodded. He looked up at the crucifix again. 'Was Mrs Florence a Christian then?'

'In a way I would say so.' He bit into his bacon roll and chewed.

'But, I don't understand. All of the stuff that she told me, about the Universe and what it can do. It doesn't sound like the kind of thing that would go down that well if I started talking about it in church.'

A big smile came across Mr Florence's face, and Jim noticed how in doing so his face resembled his wife's exactly. His cheeks pushed right up his face, so that the skin around his eyes was all bunched up and wrinkled. He laughed a little bit. 'Is that so?'

'Yeah, all that stuff about having whatever you want and asking the Universe for it. It seems kind of greedy, not very Christian at all. It feels more like casting spells and magic.'

'Ohh.' Mr Florence chuckled some more. 'Magic indeed? Spells?'

Jim looked at him, a little hurt.

'I'm sorry,' Mr Florence said. 'I'm only teasing you. I suppose you're right in a way. It does seem a bit like magic. Did you ever think that what you were doing was praying?'

Jim frowned.

'If you substituted the word Universe for God maybe?' suggested Mr Florence.

Jim was silent and tried to process what he was being told.

'Ask and it will be given to you,' Mr Florence said.

'What's that?'

'It's from the book of Matthew. You have to ask for what you want and the Universe will give it to you. Eva taught you that, didn't she?'

'Well, yeah I suppose she did.'

'Trust in the Lord with all your heart and lean not on your own understanding. That's from the book of Proverbs. Does that sound like anything my wife taught you?'

Jim thought about it. 'I suppose… Maybe the stuff about showing active faith. And maybe about viewing failures as successes. Some of the things I did didn't always make sense, but I did them anyway. And they all worked out.'

'There you go,' said Mr Florence, taking the last bite of his bacon roll.

'Why do you think Mrs Florence didn't explain it to me like that?' Jim asked.

'Like what?'

'With the Bible and all that?'

'Would you have listened to her if she had started to talk to you about the Bible?'

Jim thought. 'Probably not,' he said.

'There you go then. And the thing is, Eva didn't believe in any one religion. She thought there was a truth in all religions. Do you know what the word Islam means?'

'No.'

'It means surrender. Surrender to God. Do you know what Eva used to ask the Universe for every morning?'

Jim knew. 'Yeah,' he said. 'She used to ask one thing. To follow the Universe's plan.'

'Exactly,' said Mr Florence. 'To follow the divine plan, to surrender to it. To follow the inspiration that the Universe gave her.'

Jim smiled and nodded. That was what Mrs Florence had taught him. Quickly though, his smile turned into a frown. 'So was it part of the divine plan that she die?' The words stampeded out of him, too quick to restrain. His tone was angry, angrier than he thought it would be, and somewhat accusatory. As he looked at Mr Florence he realised that he had upset him, though he tried to hide it.

'Yes,' said Mr Florence quietly. 'It was.'

They looked at each other. Jim's facial features softened. 'I'm sorry,' he said.

'That's ok, Jim. You're still very upset.'

'Aren't you upset too?' Jim tried to say it in a way that didn't sound mean. Mr Florence looked down at his hands.

'Yes,' he said, and his hand went up to his eye to wipe something away. 'I am upset. She was the love of my life. I miss her not being there in the morning, not sitting here, in this room. I miss her laugh and her smile. Yes, I am upset. But I know that she is still here in a way. Maybe not here in her body, but here in a different way. She hasn't left me. She is still a part of the Universe.'

'But, how can you view this as a success?' Jim asked, and he felt himself begin to tear up as he said it, but managed to hold it down.

'I don't view it as a success as such. I just trust that it is right. With Eva gone, who knows what will happen next. It will be the next step in my adventure. And she'll come with me, wherever I go, in my heart. I know if I need her, she will be there for me.'

Jim thought about being hunched up at the bottom of Black Hill in complete despair over Mrs Florence no longer being there. Somehow Mr

Florence's words had soothed his mind and that fear was fading.

'I made Mrs Florence this,' Jim said, reaching into his bag and pulling out his candleholder. 'I wanted to say thank you to her for everything that she has done for me, all that she taught me, but I never got the chance to give it to her. I would like you to have it.'

'Oh Jim,' said Mr Florence. 'It's incredible. You made this yourself?'

'Yeah,' replied Jim. 'Well, with a little bit of help from the Universe of course.'

'You know, she spoke about you a lot.'

'Did she?'

'Oh yes. Every night over dinner, she would ask me how my day was and I would tell her about the flowers that were in season and the bouquets I had made for people, the special occasions they were celebrating. And then she would talk about you. You say she helped you a lot, but the truth is that you helped her a lot too.'

'I did?'

'You did. She asked the Universe for you, you know.'

'How do you mean?'

'She was bored at home. She would go out to see Steven in the mornings of course, but she wanted someone to talk to, someone who she could help in return. So she asked the Universe, and there you were, starting your first day at school. She loved having you come to visit.'

Jim was speechless. He hadn't considered that he was in some way giving something back to Mrs Florence. 'Wow,' he said eventually. 'I hadn't thought about it like that.'

'It is amazing how the Universe works, isn't it Jim? You both needed each other and there you both were, right where you needed each other. That's the divine plan for you.'

'Yeah,' said Jim, and he began to laugh. Mr Florence, seeing him laugh, joined in.

'Jim, this is a lovely gift,' he said. 'Eva would have loved it. But I think you should keep it. It is meant for you I think. Every time you light a candle in it you can think of her.'

'Ok, thanks,' said Jim, and he was pleased that he got to keep it.

'Now, let's get on with the preparations for the funeral.'

It turned out that Mr Florence needed Jim to act as a sort of secretary. His eyesight, he said, was not particularly good close up, so he wasn't able to read or write very well. While Mr Florence spoke on the phone to various people – the church, friends of Mrs Florence, the undertaker – Jim had to find the correct numbers, write down the appropriate dates, times and information. He was pleased to be of some use.

They were working in a room that Jim had not seen before, what Mr Florence called the study. There were two reading chairs with tall lamps, a strange looking desk that Mr Florence said was called a bureau and a number of bookcases lining a wall. Jim thought this was exactly like all of the studies he had ever imagined in the books that he had read. There was even a fireplace.

At one point Mr Florence was having a rather long conversation with his daughter in New Zealand, insisting that she need not come back for the funeral, it was too difficult with the children, and too expensive. Jim used this time to browse the bookshelves for he loved to read and he wondered what literature Mr and Mrs Florence read. So many of the books looked old, hardback, and thoroughly well-read; there were books and authors that Jim had heard of but never dreamed of reading – Dickens, Austen, the complete works of Shakespeare to name a few – as well as plenty that he had never heard of at all. Then there were what appeared to be religious texts too, the Bible, the Koran, and books that looked quite new, with purple covers and strange shapes on them. There was a collection of books by the Dalai Lama. Further down, in the section that Jim assumed belonged to Mr Florence, were a series of books on gardening, flowers, natural history. All of the books fascinated him, sucked him in.

'Do you enjoy reading?' asked Mr Florence, who had finished his phone conversation and turned in the chair.

'Yes,' said Jim.

'Eva used to love reading too.' He said, coming up to the bookcase. He stood with his hands on his hips and roamed the shelves with his eyes. He made humming noises with his mouth. 'Ahh,' he said. 'Here it is. Try this.'

Jim looked at the cover. It had the silhouette of a tree on it. He read the title: 'To Kill a Mockingbird by Harper Lee.' He looked at Mr Florence questioningly.

'It was one of Eva's favourites. She read that book so many times.'

'What's it about?'

'Well, I'll leave you to figure that out. You can borrow it if you want.'

'Yes, please.' Jim felt this was a gift, that after losing Mrs Florence he somehow could still hold on to her by reading this book.

'It contains a very famous quote. "You have nothing to fear but fear itself." I think that sums up a lot of what Eva taught you, doesn't it?'

Jim thought about it. 'Yes, I suppose it does. "Faith not fear" she told me once.'

'Exactly. Now, I'm very grateful for your help Jim. I wouldn't have been able to get any of this done without you reading all of the telephone numbers for me.'

'It's no problem.'

'Good lad. Would you mind stopping by some time on Monday? Just in case there is anything else that needs doing?'

'I think I should be able to do that.'

Jim said goodbye to Mr Florence mid-afternoon on Saturday. He did not go directly home but instead re-walked the route he had taken that morning in reverse. When he got to the old pillbox he stopped for a while. He perched himself on top of its flat roof and began reading the book Mr Florence had lent him. He did not mean to sit and read for as long as he did, and was shocked when he realised it was almost dinner time. He rushed home, cutting through the middle of town rather than going along the outside.

'Was everything alright with Mr Florence love?' Mum asked as he came through the door.

'Yeah, all fine.'

'Good. Well done for helping Jim. It's a nice thing to do,' Mum said, and she kissed him on the cheek. 'Sausage, chips and beans for tea.'

'Yum, thanks Mum,' Jim said, and made his way upstairs. When he got into his bedroom he cleared a small space on a shelf and on it he placed the candleholder he had made for Mrs Florence. Then he went downstairs and found a small tea light in the cupboard under the stairs. He snuck it and a box of matches back up to his room, put the tea light inside his sculpture and lit it. He stared at the figure for a time. Then he spoke.

'Dear Universe, thank you for Mrs Florence. Watch over her and protect her wherever she is. And also her husband and family.'

As he stared at the burning candle he thought about the things Mr Florence had told him. He had never thought of the Universe as being God before. Now he considered it further, he wasn't sure how he felt about it. Had Mrs Florence tricked him into believing in Christianity? He didn't think he liked the sound of that. As far as he was concerned, from what he had learnt in RE, religions were the things that stopped you from doing things for no good reason whatsoever. And after all, he thought, nobody my age believes in any of that stuff. It's all for old people.

And yet, whatever it was, whatever she had taught him, he did believe in it. He may not have seen great miracles, but his day was filled with little ones, every day, because of the Universe. He couldn't argue with that. He was a happier person because of it, and he enjoyed his life much more. He wasn't scared anywhere near as much as he used to be.

He suddenly felt like he had a lot more questions than he had ever had before. Did this mean that he should start to go to church? Was Mrs Florence in heaven? Should he start reading the Bible? It was all so confusing and he didn't have Mrs Florence to answer his questions for him. Perhaps Mr Florence might know. He would have to ask the next time he saw him.

Chapter Fourteen

Over the weekend Jim decided he wouldn't worry too much about his questions of religion until he spoke to Mr Florence again. Instead he spent a lot of his spare time reading *To Kill a Mockingbird.* He found that he didn't want to put it down and only stopped reading it for food or the odd game of PremierFoot Soccer. By the time Jim went to visit Mr Florence again on Monday he had already finished it.

'What did you think of it?' asked Mr Florence as Jim handed it back.

'It was amazing. I've never read a book like it before.'

Mr Florence smiled. 'I'm glad you liked it.'

'I could really see what Mrs Florence liked about it. And when I was reading it,' Jim hesitated, for he wasn't sure whether Mr Florence would think this sounded stupid or not. 'It was like Mrs Florence was still teaching me stuff. Which is good in a way. For a while I was worried that I had lost my teacher and everything would go wrong again.'

Mr Florence turned to him, rested one hand on his shoulder and looked him in the eye. 'Jim,' he said. 'Eva got you started, and you needed someone special like her to do that, but the Universe is your teacher. It always has been. Follow your intuition, ask the Universe for guidance and be ready to receive its lessons. Trust in it and it will always provide for you.' Mr Florence paused, turned around and picked up a photograph of Mrs Florence from the desk. 'Take me for example. I miss Eva greatly, of course I do, but already the Universe is sending me interesting new company.'

'How do you mean?' asked Jim, looking at his back questioningly. Was there already another woman in Mr Florence's life?

Mr Florence looked round at him. 'Well, you of course!' And he smiled.

'Oh, right,' said Jim, who laughed at how badly he had interpreted Mr Florence's words.

'Now, put the book back on the bookshelf for me. You can have a browse of those books whenever you like and if you see anything that draws you in then you are more than welcome to borrow it.'

'Thanks Mr Florence,' Jim replied.

'Call me Bob.'

'Ok,' said Jim, though he felt somewhat awkward about calling an adult of Mr Florence's stature by his first name.

'It's a great way of seeking guidance from the Universe that, browsing bookshelves. Eva and I used to go to the bookshops regularly and just look up and down until something popped out at us. I always found there was something in what I picked up that was what I needed to know at that time. The book was calling to me you see.'

'Yeah,' said Jim, and he smiled, because he too loved to wander bookshops, and the thought of the Universe working through them thrilled him.

'Now Jim, most things are organised for the funeral, so there isn't a lot for you to do, but I was thinking of going down to the shop today to see which flowers we might have in the church and on the coffin. Fancy coming with me?'

'Yeah, that would be brilliant!'

From Mr Florence's house, they headed down the hill that led into the high street. Mr Florence seemed very fit for his age, striding down the hill with energy. Jim was surprised, assuming that his mobility would be similar to Mrs Florence's, and he would need a walking stick of some kind.

From where they walked, high above the rest of the town, the tall church spire was visible, a symbol of Gildstow's wealth centuries earlier. Having grown up with it all his life, Jim assumed that such a thing was the norm, unaware of how scarce such architectural designs were. The church had brought the town some fame a few years earlier when a children's TV presenter had got married there. Jim remembered that some of the girls from his primary school class had stood outside to try to get a photograph, but he hadn't bothered.

'Mr Flo- sorry, Bob,' Jim said, his mind returning to his thoughts from Saturday night. 'should I go to church?'

'Why do you ask?'

'Well, it's just on Saturday you talked about how the Universe was actually God and you mentioned those bits in the Bible. So, I was just wondering if that's what I should be doing.'

'Do you want to go to church?'

'I don't think so.'

'There you go then. As I said earlier, follow your intuition and ask the Universe to guide you. That's all. I think you know this already, so stop worrying about what you think you should be doing. Maybe you'll go past a church one day and think "ooh, I might go in there," and then maybe you will. Maybe you'll wake up one morning and think "I really think I should go to church," and then maybe you will. Just ask the Universe that you follow its path and trust, Jim. Don't worry too much about the ifs and buts and shoulds. Ok?'

'Ok,' he said, and they walked the rest of the way to the shop in silence. Now that Mr Florence had said it, he felt as if this was something that he knew already. It was normal, he thought, for him to worry about what Mr Florence called the ifs and buts and shoulds. He did it all the time before he met Mrs Florence. Worrying, even after everything he had learned, was still a difficult habit to break.

Jim had walked past the yellow shop front of Florence's Florists for as long as he could remember. Not once had he given any thought to what it was or why it was there. It was just a part of the backdrop that made up the town he was growing up in. It felt strange to be walking into it now.

Mr Florence pushed the front door open and a little bell jingled above their heads. From behind the counter a young woman of about nineteen or twenty popped up.

'Ahh hello Bob!' She said.

'Hi Laura. Everything going ok?'

'Yes fine thanks. I've just finished the order for the Garrard wedding.'

'Brilliant, well done. Jim, this is Laura. She is running the shop for me at the moment, taking a year off before she starts her degree in Botany.' Laura came out from behind the counter to shake Jim's hand. 'This is Jim. He was a friend of Eva's.'

'Nice to meet you Jim,' Laura said, smiling.

'And you,' Jim replied, thinking that he was getting quite used to this shaking hands thing.

'We've just come to have a think about what flowers we might have for Eva's funeral.'

'Ahh ok,' nodded Laura. 'Let me know if I can help.' And she went back to whatever she was doing behind the counter.

Mr Florence led Jim out to the back room, which was filled to the brim with beautiful flowers of such a diverse range of shapes, sizes and colours. The smell flooded Jim's nostrils and he was reminded of sitting in the living room with Mrs Florence drinking tea.

'Right Jim,' Mr Florence said. 'I'm going to get started on the flower arrangements for the top of the coffin. I want you to pick out some flowers to be put into bouquets around the church. Does that sound alright?'

'Yeah fine,' said Jim, though he knew nothing about flowers. Mr Florence went into another room, leaving Jim by himself. Just trust, Jim said to himself. 'Dear Universe, open the way for me to choose the best flowers for Mrs Florence's funeral. I give thanks that I select them now perfectly.' Then he just stood there, in the middle of the room, for a few moments, not rushing, not panicking, not thinking. Then he started.

Immediately he felt bright and cheerful colours would be best. He saw sunflowers and chose some, beautiful, large circles of yellow joy; then he found some orange roses and grouped them alongside. Red tulips, yellow snap dragons and orange crocosmia. He wanted some green in the mixture, so included eucalyptus and fern.

'Would you like a vase to arrange them in?' Laura said, standing in the doorway.

'Yes please.' She brought him a tall glass vase with water in the bottom. 'Here you go,' she said and went back to the front of the shop.

He started to place the flowers in one at a time, picking them up randomly without thought. As the vase began to fill he noticed how they sat next to each other in a particular way; he felt he wanted a balance between all the different shapes and colours, with a variation in height so that each flower was on view and nothing overpowered anything else.

Jim stepped back and stared at it in wonder. It was glorious, beautiful, an explosion of joy and colour, and it had come from his hands. 'Thank you,' Jim whispered to the Universe. Mr Florence came into the room shortly afterwards.

'That is perfect, Jim, just perfect. Well done.'

'Thanks. I really enjoyed it.'

'Good. Shall we go and get some lunch?'

'Yeah.'

'Laura, would you take a photograph of the bouquet Jim has put together please? I would like those in the church on Friday for the funeral.'

'No problem,' said Laura, pleased to have something to do.

They walked out of the shop and down the high street to a small café. Jim ordered a tuna sandwich and lemonade, and Mr Florence had a Greek salad and a glass of water.

'How long have you been a florist?' Jim asked while they were waiting for their food.

'Well, ever since I retired really, so maybe twelve years.'

Jim nodded. 'I just remembered something I asked Mrs Florence a few weeks ago,' he said. 'We were talking about you having a job as a florist and I asked why you bothered when you could just ask the Universe for money whenever you wanted.'

A waitress came over with their drinks and they stopped talking. 'Thank you,' they said as she put them down.

'And what did Eva say?' asked Mr Florence, after the waitress had gone.

'She said that I might be able to ask you one day myself.'

'And here we are,' he said, smiling at how things had turned out. 'So, are you going to ask me?'

'Well,' said Jim. 'I think I know the answer for myself.'

'Ok, tell me.'

'You don't do it for the money. You do it because you love it. Because you enjoy putting the flowers together in lots of different ways.'

'That is exactly it Jim. When I retired, I didn't ask the Universe to give me loads of money so that I could sit around all day. In fact, it was the opposite, I asked the Universe to give me something to do that I would enjoy. The next day I strolled past this shop and there was an advert for an assistant. I got the job and then a year later the owner sold the business to me.

'It's a beautiful job, so creative. And I feel that flower arranging is a bit like a way of life. Did you notice how you instinctively tried to find variety and balance in the bouquet, that there was enough difference to make it interesting and that no one flower overpowered the rest? That's how I think life should be. Each thing that you do in life should bring you joy, just like each flower brings colour and shape to a bouquet. But too much of one type of flower, bunched together, unbalances the rest, and so it is with life too. Does that make sense?'

'Yeah, I think it makes perfect sense.'

Jim's sandwich and Mr Florence's Greek salad arrived and they ate in comfortable silence.

Chapter Fifteen

On Thursday Mum offered to take Jim out to buy a shirt and tie for the funeral. They browsed the shops separately for a short while and then met up for lunch.

'This is your first funeral Jim,' said Mum as they sat in the café. Jim nodded. 'Do you feel alright about it?'

'Yeah, I think so,' he replied. He felt as if he had grown up quite a lot over the last few months - secondary schools, handshakes and funerals.

'Because I can come with you if you want, you know, for a bit of support.'

'Maybe,' said Jim. He was grateful that Mum had offered, but part of him felt like this was something that he wanted to do himself. His friendship with Mrs Florence was a side of who he was that was independent to his mum. It was unusual in this way. Anybody he had any kind of proper relationship with, his mum knew as well. Family members, school friends – his parents had an influence over his view of all of them. But not Mrs Florence. 'I'll have a think about it. Thanks though,' he said, after some musing.

'It was nice of Mr Florence to let you help out with the flowers. You've been working hard to sort those out,' Mum said. Jim had been working hard. Laura had asked for an extra pair of hands to help get the flowers ready, so on Wednesday he had spent the whole day in the shop helping to sort them out.

'Yeah, should be really nice Mum,' said Jim. 'I quite enjoy flower arranging. All the different shapes and colours of the petals. It's interesting.'

'It sounds like a good experience anyway Jim.'

'Yeah.'

After they had finished their lunches, Jim took his mum to show her the shirt and tie he liked.

'I was thinking about this one,' he said, holding up a tie.

'You can't wear that to a funeral Jim,' Mum said.

'Why not?'

'Well, it's bright pink! Funerals are sad occasions. You're supposed to wear black.'

'But why?'

'Because it's sad. You wear black to show you are in mourning.'

But Jim was adamant. He had thought about what Mr Florence had said about browsing bookshops. He hadn't had the chance that morning to go into a bookshop and see if the Universe would call out at him from a book, but he thought he would try it with buying a shirt and tie instead. And there it was, shouting out to him from the racks, a beautiful bright pink tie. He couldn't help thinking that Mrs Florence would have loved it. He had seen her wearing similar colours on some occasions when he had gone to visit her, and he knew that wherever she was, she would appreciate it.

'Well, ok,' said Mum. 'If you are sure that's what you want, I'll buy it for you.' He decided that the tie would sit best next to a white shirt, so they bought one of those too and then headed home.

'You know Jim,' said Mum, a bit later on that day. 'I think I'm starting to quite like that tie you bought.'

'Thanks Mum,' he said.

The day of the funeral came. Mum had ironed his shirt and hung it on his wardrobe door, ready for use. As it was an important day, Mum had also made him a bacon sandwich for breakfast so that he wouldn't feel so hungry later on. She wasn't sure, she had said, if the funeral would go through lunch.

Jim got dressed, tying his tie with far more ease than he would have done six or seven weeks earlier. He checked himself in the mirror to ensure that he looked smart. 'Are you sure you don't want me to come with you?' Mum called from downstairs. 'No, I'm fine thanks,' he called back. Then, about eleven o'clock, he began to walk down to the church.

It was a drizzly day and Jim had to wear his waterproof jacket over his shirt and tie. He walked down to the high street, as this was the quickest way to the church, and found it busy with traffic and people going about their daily business. He found this a strange sensation. While he was going to mark the end of somebody's life, so many other people were doing what they always did on a Friday, perhaps going to the bank, doing some shopping, sending something at the post office. Life, he thought, keeps going.

He turned off the high street and walked towards the church with its high spire. It was a special place, he knew. Surrounded on either side by two graveyards, with a protective wall of other town buildings enveloping it from a distance, it was set off from the roads, a little island of peace. It was old too; much like the rest of the town it seeped with history, though Jim had no real idea how many years it had been since it was built.

He walked in through the church entrance and found that a few others had already arrived and were sat waiting in the pews. Standing just inside the entrance were Mr Florence and another man, perhaps around his dad's age. As he looked at them he knew he had made the right choice in wearing the pink tie. Mr Florence was wearing a deep red colour and the other man a light purple. No black here, Jim thought.

'Ahh Jim,' said Mr Florence. 'It's brilliant to have you here. Thank you for coming.' He took Jim's hand and shook it. 'This is our son, Steven,' he said, motioning to the man standing next to him. Initially, Jim couldn't recognise features of Mr and Mrs Florence in the man's face, so thin and worn did it look, and in some strange way he looked older, more tired, than Mr Florence did. But as Steven extended his hand towards Jim and Jim took it in return, he saw Mr Florence in his eyes and Mrs Florence in his smile.

'It's nice to meet you Jim,' he said. 'My mum told me all about you.'

'It's nice to meet you too,' said Jim, finding it odd to hear Mrs Florence referred to as mum.

'Your flowers look amazing. Thanks for helping Dad with those.'

'Oh,' said Jim, looking around to see if he could spot them. 'I was happy to. I enjoyed it.'

'They're just round there,' said Steven, pointing round to the main aisle of the church. 'Nice tie by the way,' he said, winking and smiling.

'Thanks,' said Jim and walked to go down the central aisle of the church. The old wooden pews lined either side of the aisle and next to those, intermittently, were tall stone columns that went up to a ceiling as tall as Jim's house. They were amazing feats of architecture, he thought. Considering they were built at a time without machinery, such buildings had always filled him with a great sense of wonder.

Adorning each column, on either side, his bouquets radiated with glory. They were floral fires of love and joy, in precession all the way to the front of the church. Jim was so pleased with how they looked, he almost wished his mum had been there so that he could show her what he had done.

He found a seat somewhere in the middle of the church, on an empty pew. There were maybe thirty or forty other people there. Jim was the youngest by a long way and didn't know anybody else, but this didn't matter to him: somehow he knew that Mrs Florence was there with him, he could feel it in his heart. And far from it being a sad occasion, Jim knew this was a celebration of her life, and it filled him with joy. It was a new sensation inside of him, not like a brief happiness at having got the thing you want, but more like a warm burning of a home fire in his stomach, in his heart. It was a knowing, a certainty, that Mrs Florence was still part of the Universe and always would be. It was faith, not fear, and it seemed to bubble up every now and again and made him want to laugh.

Mr Florence and Steven sat down at the front of the church, as did a few others who were milling around at the back. The priest, with his long robes of white and black, came and stood at the lectern, just in front of the coffin. Jim recognised him. He often came to his primary school to lead assemblies or run activities.

The priest welcomed everyone to the church and introduced himself. He said that they were here to remember Eva and celebrate her life, which is exactly what Jim had thought. 'We will start with our first hymn,' the priest said, and everyone stood up. Jim sang. He didn't know the tune very well and he wasn't that sure he understood the words he was singing, even though they were in English, but he sang anyway. He felt that it was only right.

Steven stood up and gave a reading from the Bible next. Jim, surprisingly, recognised it. It included the quotation that Mr Florence had told him about – ask and you shall receive – from the Book of Matthew. He smiled to himself and listened to every word.

Steven read calmly, with a clarity and a quiet confidence; Jim wondered about his life. How had he become addicted to drugs? Was he completely better now? He seemed well from what Jim saw, but then what did he know – he wasn't a doctor after all.

The reading finished and there was another song, 'Give Me Oil in My Lamp', which Jim recognised from primary school singing practices, and he made a point of singing this as loud as he could. Some of the ladies in the row in front of him picked up on his enthusiasm and also began to sing their hearts out.

There was another reading, this time by Mr Florence. It was a psalm, 'The Lord is My Shepherd', which Jim also recognised. When he finished reading he raised his hand to his lips, kissed it and then blew the kiss in the direction of the coffin. He loved her, of course. Jim wondered what they would have been like together, how they would have interacted. He imagined them holding hands a lot, joking with each other – lots of laughing.

Then the priest stood up and said that it was time for the eulogy. Jim wasn't sure what that was, but soon found out it was a sort of story of her life.

'Well,' the priest began. 'You all know Eva, of course. You know her as an incredibly loving woman, very helpful, very kind. She never had a bad word to say about anyone and she was always happy to see anybody at any time. She was a woman of great faith (I sometimes thought she was of greater faith than me) and had a deep trust in God.

'Eva Florence was born Eva Penrose in 1932 in Padstow in Cornwall,' the priest began to tell the history of her life. Jim listened avidly. 'She was the youngest of three sisters. Her father was a fisherman, and Eva suffered the first great sorrow of her life when he tragically died at sea in 1939. Her mother at this time began to suffer from depression and Eva and her two older sisters were sent to live with a friend of the family in Boscastle. Eva referred to her as Aunty Elizabeth, though she wasn't a blood relative. Eva told me once that she gained her deep faith in God from this Elizabeth, who she said taught her everything she knew.

'Following the death of her father, Eva had a relatively quiet upbringing, visiting her mother whenever possible and working hard at school. When she was old enough, however, she quickly became independent and this appears to have been encouraged by Aunty Elizabeth. She exercised her faith when she moved to London at the age of nineteen, with no job waiting for her and little money. She simply said that she felt this was the right thing to do. And indeed it was, for it was on the platform of Paddington station, where her train pulled in for the first time, that she met her future husband, Robert. The story goes that Eva's suitcase broke right in front of Robert and all of her clothes tumbled onto the floor in front of him.' Some laughter from the congregation could be heard at this point. Jim laughed too. 'And Robert stopped and helped her pick them up. How's that for divine intervention!' Some more, brief laughter.

'Three weeks later Robert asked Eva to marry him, and she immediately said yes. Asked later on why she had agreed to his proposal so quickly, ever the romantic, Eva said that once he had seen her undergarments on the first day they met, she had few other secrets to keep from him.' Another chuckle from the congregation.

'They married quickly and have had what Robert describes as over fifty beautiful years together. Unusually for the time, they decided not to have children straight away. Instead a series of fortuitous job opportunities for Robert meant that they were able to travel the world, living in India, Hong Kong and Egypt, to name a few. Eva once described those years as part of life's beautiful adventure. She loved the travel, the learning about new cultures and the meeting new people, and she did all of these things fearlessly.

'Eventually they did return home to the UK, however, and they moved here to Gildstow, where they had two children, Becky and Steven, and settled here for some time. Eva said that becoming a mother was the greatest adventure of all.

'In her later years, Eva became a grandmother to two girls, Elizabeth and Sarah. Becky had emigrated to New Zealand with her partner, and she and Robert decided to move out there as well to spend as much time with their grandchildren as possible. Last year they returned to Gildstow to spend more time with their son, Steven, and manage their florist business more easily.

'Far from being a disappointment after spending so much time in the pacific climes of New Zealand, Eva said a couple of weeks before she died that she loved living back in Gildstow. She was so pleased to spend time with her son again, having developed in this last year a closer, more beautiful relationship than before, but she also spoke of the new friendships that had come into her life that brought her great happiness.

'Eva Florence, I'm sure you'll agree, was greatly loved and will be greatly missed.' He paused while everyone reflected on these words. 'It's time for our final hymn,' he said.

Jim didn't recognise the final song either, but it was happy and uplifting, and he did his best to sing along with energy and enthusiasm. He felt himself being swept along on a wave of – what was it? Happiness? Freedom? Love? He had seen funerals in films before. The way he felt was not the way they appeared to feel on screen, those sobbing, tissue-clutching sufferers. Was it wrong that he wasn't upset – heartbroken even – at this event marking Mrs Florence's death?

It didn't feel wrong. It felt as if Mrs Florence was here, with him. Not in the sense that he felt her standing next to him; more it was a feeling inside.

'Eva requested,' said the priest, after the hymn had finished. 'that we conclude her funeral with the Lord's prayer, so if we say together, Our Father, who art in heaven...' The congregation joined in. '...thy kingdom come, thy will be done...' Jim also joined in. '...Give us this day our daily bread and forgive us our trespasses...' He had said it so many times before without really thinking about the words; his primary school, which was linked with the church, often got the pupils to recite it during assemblies or at other events. '...but deliver us from evil...' It was a strange thing, he thought, to observe. There was something robotic about the delivery of the words. And yet Mrs Florence wanted it said, so perhaps there was something to it after all.

At the end of the funeral, the priest announced that there would be a wake in the town hall and that all would be welcome. Jim wasn't sure what a wake was, but he decided to go. He watched the coffin being carried out of the church, Steven and Mr Florence bearing the weight at the front. It seemed as if Steven caught his eye as he went past, and Jim was sure that he gave him a smile.

Jim smiled back. He wanted to speak to Steven, find out more about him, yet he felt intimidated by him too. He knew so very little about him, but what he did know was not positive. Drug addiction was a big scary adult world idea that made him want to run to his bedroom and hide under his duvet. And he still couldn't understand how such a thing could happen to Steven when he had a mother like Mrs Florence. It wasn't the kind of question you could ask though. Jim knew that it was highly impolite to pry about people's dark pasts.

Jim stood outside the church. There was a gentle stream of funeral attendees making their way past the graveyard and along the path towards the town hall, and he joined in with the flow, tagging on at the end. A few people glanced at him in a curious but harmless manner, obviously wondering why he, so young and not a relative, had attended.

'May I join you?' Someone asked from behind. Jim turned to see the priest following along.

'Yes, alright then.' The priest came alongside and fell into step with Jim.

'How did you know Eva?' He asked.

'I walked past her house on the way home from school,' said Jim. 'She used to give me tea and biscuits.'

'Ahh,' said the priest, smiling. 'That sounds very much like Eva.'

'Yeah,' said Jim. 'Did she come to church a lot?'

'Sometimes. I know it might seem wrong for me to say this, but I always felt someone like Eva didn't need to come to church. She carried God in her heart.'

'Yeah,' said Jim. He felt there was some truth in that. 'Can I ask you a question?'

'Of course.'

'Why do you wear all black?'

'Haha, it's a good question! It does seem like quite a gloomy outfit, doesn't it? Different people in the church wear different colours, but parish priests tend to wear black. I think it symbolises poverty.'

'Poverty?'

'As in, you don't really get into priesthood for the money. You do it to spread the word of God.' He offered a broad grin and Jim noticed that the priest was a lot younger than he had originally thought.

They entered the town hall and a woman, seemingly a regular attendee of the church, accosted the priest, leaving Jim to his own devices. He moved over to the refreshments table, where he was offered a cup of tea and, much to his delight, some custard creams. There were lots of small round tables with chairs and Jim picked one in the corner.

He considered his brief conversation with the priest. He found the black clothes a silly choice. Surely, he thought, they should be bright colours to show how happy you are to have that relationship with God. Weird too, he thought, to think that your relationship with God makes you poor. When he first started to understand what Mrs Florence meant by the Universe, his relationship with it suddenly made him feel incredibly rich, as if nothing was out of his reach and he would never be in need of anything again.

That was Jim's big issue with going to church. He agreed with the principle, and perhaps God and the Universe were the same thing, but there were these rules and ideas that didn't ring true for him. At least for now.

One thing that did seem right though, was the Lord's prayer. In the past, at his primary school, Jim had only given one word much thought – trespasses. He felt it was a funny thing to ask forgiveness for, particularly considering his parents had insisted from an early age that he never trespassed. What about all those other sins, Jim thought, that I might need forgiveness for?

Yet the Lord's prayer seemed to have some similarities with Mrs Florence's teachings. 'Thy will be done' reminded Jim of her request to 'follow the Universe's path'; he found the 'give us this day our daily bread' a demand, much like Mrs Florence had taught him to say if he wanted something. In fact, the whole prayer was a list of demands to God. There was something about it that Jim quite liked, and in his mind, as he munched on his custard cream he began to form his own daily prayer – a prayer to the Universe.

'Alright Jim,' said Steven, interrupting his thoughts. He pulled up a chair next to him and sat, cup of tea in hand.

'Hi Steven. Did everything go ok at the cemetery?'

'Yes thanks, all fine. Mum has a nice little plot up there overlooking the cricket ground. We put some of your flowers on the grave.'

'That's good,' said Jim.

'I've been meaning to thank you, you know.'

'Me?'

'Yeah. You helped my mum and me a lot.'

'I did?'

'You did. You were just the right person at just the right time my friend. Mum would call that synchronicity. You see, Mum was coming to see me at the centre every day, and I was getting better. I knew that we were building a bond that hadn't been as strong in the last few years, but the problem was, with me Mum found it difficult to trust in the Universe. She told me this herself. I guess it was just a mother's instinct. If there is one thing you fear for, it is your child. She was desperate to help me and worried perhaps too much. I could feel it and it started to put strain on our relationship again.

'She knew it too. And she did try, but she needed something else. So she asked the Universe and you came along. The right person at the right time.'

'What did I do?'

'Well, she wanted to help me, but really she had to let go. Let go of her fear and have faith. When you started visiting Mum, it gave her someone else to help, to put her energies into. And in teaching you the things she did, she was reminded of the things she needed to do herself, for me. And so when she came to see me, instead of constantly asking me how I was, she started talking about you, and our relationship properly healed, and I healed too. By being there to be helped, you were helping her, and, actually, me. So thank you,' he said. And he held out his hand for Jim to shake, which he did.

'Wow,' said Jim. 'That's amazing.'

'Isn't it?' Steven gave a broad smile.

Jim decided to have faith, not fear, and ask the question he had been wondering. 'Steven, do you mind me asking, how did you...' But he couldn't find the words.

Steven finished them for him. 'End up in a rehabilitation centre?'

'Yeah.'

'It's hard to explain without making it sound like I'm blaming my mum. I'm not. We are all human after all, and even someone with a deep faith like hers can be fearful sometimes. And she was fearful about me, even from when I was a little boy. I think it was partly because I was her youngest child and partly because I was a boy and seemed to have a tendency to be a bit wild. So she kept me closer than Becky, was more fearful of me hurting myself, so tried harder to protect me.

'By the time I got to my teenage years, I began to find the whole thing far too claustrophobic. The whole Universe stuff – I didn't buy into it. I started to rebel – alcohol, then cannabis. And the more I rebelled, the more Mum tried to pull me closer, and so the more I rebelled. I wasn't a very nice son.'

Steven paused for a moment and considered what he had just said. He had become very solemn. 'It's a bit more complicated than that, of course, but that's the crux of it. Things just spiralled. I moved out as soon as I could. Ended up in with a bad lot. Moved out of Gildstow to London. Started committing crimes to pay for drugs. Every now and then I would show up on Mum and Dad's doorstep with the intention of getting some money, and they would give it to me because they loved me…

'Then one day they just let go. They moved to New Zealand to live with Becky and suddenly that overprotection I had always felt stifling me was now completely gone. That's when I felt like I woke up. It wasn't stifling, it was love, and it had disappeared to the other side of the planet.

'It took me a little while to get out of the situation I was in, of course. Years. But I did it. Finally got myself into a rehab centre and that was when I called Mum and Dad. I said I missed them and Dad said they had some issues with the florist shop that they needed to come home to sort anyway, so they came back. And here we are.'

Jim swallowed, unsure of what to say. There was a silence.

'So anyway,' said Steven, suddenly becoming more cheerful. 'I owe you my thanks,' and he placed his hand on Jim's shoulder and gave it a little shake in a gesture of gratitude.

'Er… no problem?'

Steven laughed. 'I'm going to start living with Dad now, help out at the florist shop and so on. Come and see us whenever you like, ok?'

'That would be good,' said Jim.

It was getting on for dinner time and Jim was feeling very hungry. He said his goodbyes to Steven, Mr Florence and the priest and made his way home. As he walked he considered what Steven had told him. It was a surprise that someone as wise and as faithful as Mrs Florence had also had her moments of fear. It made Jim view his own mother differently; he decided he would try his best to appreciate her overprotectiveness a bit more, rather than get annoyed with her.

He felt good that he had been of some help to Mrs Florence and to Steven, but he couldn't help considering how much of an impact Steven had had on his life. After all, if he hadn't rebelled and started taking drugs and so on, he would never have ended up in the rehabilitation centre. Mrs Florence might never have come back from New Zealand and he would never have met her. So should he have been thanking Steven? For going through all those bad things? It seemed complicated. Perhaps he was worrying about it too much.

He walked through the back door of his house and Mum was in the kitchen preparing dinner. She walked up to him, held his face in her hands and tenderly kissed his cheek. 'How was it?'

'Yeah it was fine thanks Mum. I actually quite enjoyed it.'

'Did you?' Mum replied, a slight tone of surprise in her voice. 'Ok, well, go and get changed. Dinner will be ready in a minute. It's shepherd's pie.'

'Yes! Thanks Mum,' said Jim, bounding up the stairs.

Chapter Sixteen

Jim spent most of Saturday at Tom's house playing computer games. Before he knew it the weekend was gone and he was back at school on Monday morning. These November days were shorter, colder and darker, but he did not mind and was quite excited about Fireworks Night and the build up to Christmas. Jim loved Christmas, and however he felt about his parents and their arguments, he knew they always had an excellent Christmas day.

Jim was aware - he had not forgotten - as he hung around the playground on that drizzly Monday, that Mrs Florence would not be there waiting for him on his way home, but he did not mind this either. For one thing, he thought that, perhaps if he timed it correctly, he might see Steven, who he had become quite fond of since the wake, or indeed Mr Florence, waiting with a cup of tea on those wintry evenings. But more than this, something of the fire that had burned in him during the funeral remained still, so he did not feel that he had lost her. In a way, he felt as if it was his responsibility to continue something – the things that Mrs Florence did – to help those around him. Not necessarily to start telling people about the

Universe; he understood that some people might not be ready for it, but to spread the happiness, the faith and not the fear. That was Jim's plan for now on.

He stood in the playground alone. As yet, none of his mates had arrived. It was odd, as often most of them were here by this time, but for Jim it was perfect. He said 'Dear Universe, put me in positions where I can successfully help people this day. Spread happiness and faith through me to those I meet today.'

Then Jim went and sat on a bench and waited. Slowly pupils were arriving into the playground, their feet dragging their bodies reluctantly onto the school grounds. Eventually Tom and a couple of the other boys showed up, and in no time at all this felt like any other Monday morning they had had at the school so far, just wetter and colder.

Jim found himself presented with his first opportunity to help someone during lesson one. It was English, and the teacher had put them into a new seating plan, 'to keep you on your toes,' he had said, which was interesting because they were sat down. The seating plan was boy-girl-boy-girl and Jim had been placed next to a rather quiet nervous girl called Lucy.

'I'd like you to read this poem. What do you think it's about? Discuss it with the person next to you,' the teacher, Mr Simpson, said when the lesson had started and the class were settled.

Jim and Lucy read the poem in silence. It was called 'The Schoolboy' and was by a poet called

William Blake. Eventually, after enough time had elapsed, Jim asked 'what do you think it's about?'

Lucy simply gave a shy smile and shrugged her shoulders. Jim performed his best uncertain expression. He wondered how he might encourage Lucy to say something, but didn't want to make her feel uncomfortable. Then he remembered what Steven had said at the wake, about how by helping Jim Mrs Florence was also helping herself. 'Can you help me Lucy? I don't think I've got the faintest idea what this poem is about, and Mr Simpson always picks on me.'

Lucy offered a pensive look. 'I think,' she said quietly, pointing to some words in the poem. 'I think he is saying that the schoolboy is like the bird in the cage.'

'What, like trapped?'

'Yeah. And he's saying that when you are trapped like that you can't be happy. Like the bird singing…' All the time that she spoke she did not look him in the eyes.

'Ahh, ok. That makes a lot of sense, thanks.'

'Right everybody,' said Mr Simpson from the front of the class. 'This way please.' He waited for the class to settle down. 'Who can tell me what this poem is about?'

The room was silent. 'Well, there was a lot of chatter just now. One of you must have some idea.' Nobody put a hand up. Everyone sat still: some with pursed, inquisitive looks, as if they were diligently trying to figure out the answer to the question; some looking down at the table in front of them; some doing their very best impression of a mannequin. The clock ticked and, while it was only a matter of seconds that passed, it seemed longer.

Jim put his hand up. 'Yes Jim,' Mr Simpson said, relieved that someone had volunteered.

'Well,' said Jim, 'I didn't really get it until Lucy explained it to me.'

'Oh right, and what did Lucy say?'

'She said that you can't be happy when you feel trapped, just like a bird can't sing in a cage. And the schoolboy is the bird.'

'That's an excellent answer. Thank you for sharing Jim, and well done Lucy for such a brilliant idea.'

The rest of the lesson passed without much event. The teacher talked them through the poem and they had to annotate it, then answer some questions. Jim enjoyed it because he felt he could apply the meaning to what he had learned from Mrs Florence. The cage, as far as Jim was concerned, wasn't simply a classroom, it was a person's own fear. When a person has faith, that cage dissolves and they realise they were free all along.

At break time Jim was on his way to the canteen to buy a snack when Lucy caught up with him. 'Hi Jim,' she said.

'Hi,' said Jim. He smiled, he thought, perhaps in a similar way to Mrs Florence, though he wasn't sure if he was just coming across as a bit creepy. There was a silence between them and Jim felt he should fill the space. 'Thanks for your help back there in English.'

'That's alright,' she said, and she smiled a little bit too. Her eyes were brown. It seemed as if she was on the verge of saying something but was too shy to do so.

'It seems like Mr Simpson was really pleased with your idea,' said Jim, to help the conversation along.

'Yeah,' said Lucy, and then, as if finally committing to diving into a pool, 'thanks for telling him.' And it seemed as if relief blossomed on her face as she spoke.

'That's alright. I thought it was a good idea but didn't want to take the credit.'

One of Lucy's friends was waving her over from across the canteen.

'Well, thanks anyway,' said Lucy as she got up and walked over to her friends.

'No problem.' Jim felt satisfied that he had done at least one good thing for the day. He found himself feeling excited about it too. He felt as if he was a spy, sent from the Universe, to carry out this simple mission of helping others; and school, though he was happy to admit he found it interesting, would be so much the more interesting now he had an ulterior motive for being there.

Jim found his second opportunity to help someone during the second lesson. It was history, which he had always really enjoyed as a subject, but since joining high school he felt that he hadn't been learning as much. The problem was that his class was very naughty; it was strange, as they (more or less) behaved for all the other teachers, but with their history teacher, Mr Ashoka, they were often unruly.

Jim put it down to two main reasons. Firstly, and perhaps less significantly, was the fact that Mr Ashoka had a strong Indian accent. The class, who had inexperienced ears, found it difficult to understand Mr Ashoka's instructions. Then boys like Greg and Dominic would secretly mock the way that he said things, surreptitiously mimicking his voice at the back of the classroom. The class would burst into laughter, and Mr Ashoka, who hadn't heard what had been said, was at a loss as to how to regain control.

The second reason was that, as far as Jim could tell, Mr Ashoka was a relatively new teacher. He seemed quite young and demonstrated all of the signs of inexperience. It wasn't necessarily the fact that he didn't know the answers to their questions, or he didn't appear to be that well organised, it was that he entirely lacked confidence. There were other teachers in the school who were just as disorganised and also didn't seem to know everything about the subject they were teaching, but they exuded a confidence, and that is what made the difference to how well they could control a class. He had fear, rather than faith, and the class played on that.

They were covering a history of Britain, and had already looked at the Romans and then the Saxons in their first half term. Jim was disappointed that they had not started their history lessons at an earlier point in time, as he was fascinated by the Bronze Age and Stonehenge after his parents had taken him to Wiltshire during the summer holidays. This lesson was supposed to be about the Vikings, but Greg and Dominic were up to their normal shenanigans and it seemed that, no matter what Mr Ashoka tried, the class were reluctant to learn.

At the end of the lesson, the class were filtering out of the room and Mr Ashoka slumped into his chair, head in his hands. It was only the second lesson of the half term and he already looked exhausted. Jim spotted his opportunity to spread some happiness.

'Mr Ashoka,' he said, quietly shuffling up to the desk.

Mr Ashoka looked up from his hands, somewhat surprised. 'Er, yes Jim?'

'I just wanted to say thank you for the lesson.' Mr Ashoka looked at him, one eyebrow raised. Jim felt compelled to continue. 'I found it really interesting and really enjoyed the activity with all of the coloured cards. That must have taken ages to do.'

'Oh, well,' said Mr Ashoka, blustering a little with surprise. 'Thank you very much,' he continued, his face lighting up and washing away the fatigue. 'I'm glad you liked it.'

'Yeah, I did.' Jim said. 'See you next lesson.' And he walked out of the class.

He grinned as he left. It was that moment of transformation on their faces, both Lucy's and Mr

Ashoka's, that made him so happy. It was the visible change of fear into faith.

At lunchtime he was presented with another chance to help somebody. A group of year seven boys were on the field playing football, as they always did whenever they had the chance. Sometimes it was too wet and the headteacher, Mr Gostling, would close the field, leaving swathes of social groups to wander, nomadic, from one spot to another, searching for some form of entertainment. Today, however, despite the drizzle, Mr Gostling gave permission for it to be open.

There was a specific place that the year seven boys played. It was an unspoken rule that the year eleven boys played football in the top left corner of the field, the furthest point from teacher supervision, where rumour had it that they would attempt to hide behind the trees to smoke. The year ten boys had the top right corner, the nines in the middle, the eights bottom right and the sevens bottom left. It was fair to say the year sevens had the worst patch of land to play on, so close as it was to the school buildings and other obstructions, such as the long jump sandpit. Nonetheless, it was their spot and they were happy to have it.

The match was going well and Jim's side were 2-1 up. Then Dominic, who had a tendency to be both foolish and irritating, booted the ball towards the top left hand corner of the pitch. He was forced by his fellow players to run and get it, at which point a year eleven boy was also running to get his ball. There was some confusion, and, when asked afterwards how it had happened, no one could really remember. Suffice to say there was a collision. The year eleven boy, who was more man than boy in physicality, shoved Dominic to the ground and made some threatening gesture towards him with his fists. Jim, who was nearby, saw this and ran over to help. As he drew closer, the size of the year eleven boy became obvious, but it did not dissuade him. Repeating the words 'faith not fear' in his head, he walked up to Dominic and held out a hand to help him up, saying 'Are you alright Dominic?'

The year eleven boy was somewhat taken aback by this boldness on the part of some unknown year seven, and was initially slow to react. Dominic, on the other hand, so thoroughly embarrassed at being seen to be in a position of weakness, got up by himself and shoved Jim onto the ground, saying 'get lost Jim!' The year eleven boy finally clocked what had happened, burst out laughing at this pantomime of antics and ran back to his friends to relay the event.

Jim lay on the floor for a moment or two, surprised by what had just occurred. As he raised himself onto his elbows he saw Dominic being chastised by the other year sevens for pushing him over. Had this occurred two or three months ago, he thought, he would have been really upset by what had happened. Perhaps he wouldn't have gone on the field again, or even bothered to play football at all, choosing instead to hang around in the library every lunchtime. But today, knowing all that he did, Jim felt an overwhelming desire to laugh at the whole situation. He pulled himself to his feet and jogged back over to the game with an amused look on his face. 'Are you alright Jim?' a couple of the boys asked as he rejoined them.

'Yeah fine, ta,' he chuckled. 'Absolutely fine.'

On the way home (John was going round Jennifer's), Jim walked past Mr and Mrs Florence's house. He had wondered if he might be able to stop in to see Steven and Mr Florence, but all the lights were off and it was clear that nobody was home. He assumed they were still at the florist shop, and thought that perhaps tomorrow or the next day he might walk that way home so that he might pop in and say hello.

Instead, as he walked down the hill towards his house, he pondered on all that had happened that day. It was curious that Dominic had reacted the way he had. Some people, he thought, just aren't ready to be helped. Or maybe they are just too scared to receive help. In his mind, he thought it was similar to what had happened between Steven and Mrs Florence. Steven wasn't ready to be helped at the time and, as he had said himself, he wasn't a very nice son.

Nonetheless, Jim noticed a rapid change in Lucy and Mr Ashoka. The next day in English, Lucy put her hand up three times to share her ideas, which thrilled Mr Simpson, who thought they were 'absolutely superb.' Jim found Lucy was becoming more and more talkative in their paired work too, telling him all about the metaphors and rhyme scheme that the poet had used. It was brilliant. Jim felt like he was understanding far more about poetry than he ever had.

'Yesterday,' he said to Lucy as they were walking out of the classroom, 'you were thanking me for telling Mr Simpson your idea, but I think it's me that should be thanking you now. I would have been lost in that lesson without you there to tell me what was going on!'

'That's alright,' said Lucy. 'I enjoyed it.'

The effect on Mr Ashoka was similarly positive. There was something about him that seemed more confident, less uncertain about what he was doing there, and that, in turn, meant that the pupils seemed more willing to go along with what he said. At the back of the class Greg and Dominic attempted to mock his accent once, but were quickly reprimanded by Mr Ashoka, who asked them whether they did impressions of all of their teachers. The boys became sheepish when they realised that they might be accused of racism and settled into a grumpy silence for the rest of the lesson. Jim, along with the rest of the class, suddenly felt far happier to be in the classroom.

Jim's secret mission to help others was an immediately fruitful enterprise and he loved to see the effect small actions of kindness could have on the people around him. He thought of it in terms of how Mr Florence had described life – as another beautiful flower within his bouquet that brought new colour and shape.

Chapter Seventeen

The next day, walking home from school, Jim had a big surprise. He had turned the corner of Black Hill, exited the alleyway that led onto Mrs Florence's road (for he still thought of it as her road) and was taken aback by what he saw outside her house (for he still thought of it as her house). He stood and stared in a state of shock before running straight up to the front door and knocking. It did not take long before Mr Florence came to the door.

'Jim!' he said, a hint of surprise in his voice. 'How nice to see you! I'm sorry, I was expecting someone else. Come on through.'

Jim moved into the living room and sat down in his normal chair. His brows were knitted. 'Are you… moving?' He asked. He was referring to the estate agents sign that stood outside, hammered into Mrs Florence's lawn.

Mr Florence rubbed his chin and face in contemplation of the best way to explain. He breathed out heavily, sat down and began to speak – 'well, the thing is Jim,' – before there was another knock at the door and he jumped back up again. 'Sorry, I just have to get this.'

Jim remained seated in the living room while Mr Florence went to answer the door. 'Ahh hello,' Jim heard him say. 'Mr and Mrs Edwards, is it? It's lovely to meet you. Come on through.' A couple, probably in their forties, stood in the hallway. 'Well, this is the hallway,' said Mr Florence, and then, leading them through into the room Jim was sat in, 'and this is the living room.' The couple, as they were being shown around, made statements like 'isn't it lovely?' and 'ooh yes.' Jim could sense as they looked around that they were already considering the changes they would make – the paintwork, the carpets, maybe knock a wall through.

Mr Florence led the couple through to the kitchen and then up the stairs, and Jim was left to sit by himself. He felt a pang of jealousy. He knew the room did not belong to him, but so much of who he now viewed himself to be was created in this room, and he wasn't sure that he was ready to let it go. He stared at the paintings of seaside villages, fishing boats; he stared at the diverse religious symbols around the room, seemingly in conflict and yet somehow hanging in perfect harmony. He sat back in his chair, felt his feet on the carpet and tried to in some way engrave this image into his mind so that he could come back to it whenever he needed to. And in his mind's eye he placed Mrs Florence in the chair opposite him too, so that there, in his memory, she would always be for advice and guidance.

He heard the voices, muffled through the ceiling, upstairs. The man laughed at something the woman said as they moved from bedroom to bedroom. Jim thought about leaving; he remembered Mr Florence's surprise when he opened the door to see him instead of the people who had come to buy the house and suddenly felt like he shouldn't be there at all; he felt as if he had no place there at all, that he was foolish to believe that he did. He listened to the voices above and calculated how far they were from the stairway; perhaps he could sneak out now and avoid any embarrassing exit; he would have to leave now though, otherwise it would be too late. Just get up and walk out now and no one will see.

Stop. Faith, not fear Jim.

He paused. His mind had overrun. He felt for a short time as if he was the old Jim, Jim the worrier. He sat back down in the chair and closed his eyes, took long, deep breaths in and out of his belly. He had allowed fear to take control, but not now. Now he would trust in the Universe. Faith, not fear, he repeated to himself.

He became aware of footsteps coming down the stairs. 'If you have any questions at all,' he heard Mr Florence saying. 'Don't hesitate to pop round and ask.'

The Edwards were overflowing with politeness as they thanked him and said goodbye. Mr Florence opened the front door and showed them out. The door closed. 'Are you alright Jim?' He asked.

Jim opened his eyes. 'Yes, better now thanks.'

'Can I make you a cup of tea?'

'Please.'

Moments later, Mr Florence returned with two mugs and some custard creams. He handed Jim the mug with the New Zealand birds on it. 'Thanks,' Jim said.

Mr Florence settled down into his chair, slipped off his slippers and put his feet up on a footstool. 'I'm sorry you had to find out we were leaving just like that Jim. I wanted to talk to you first, but the estate agent came and put the sign up while we were at the shop this morning. I didn't even know we were officially on the market until I got a phone call telling me we had a viewing this afternoon.'

'That's alright. I was a bit surprised at first, but I was just overreacting.' Jim blew on his tea and took a sip. 'Where do you think you are going to move to?'

'Well, Steven and I have been talking and we have decided to move out to New Zealand, so that we are closer to Becky and the girls. It will be a new start for Steven... a new start for both of us really. Do you remember when you asked me how I could view Eva's death as a success? And I said that I didn't view it like that, but I trusted that it was the right thing to have happened, and that it would open an opportunity for the next thing? Well, this is that next thing - the next step in my adventure. Do I miss Eva? Of course, every day. But this is the next step. We couldn't have any beginnings if we didn't have any endings.'

'Yeah, I guess that makes sense... Do you think Mrs Florence is in heaven?'

'I don't know for certain, but I like to think she is somewhere like that. But then I guess the question is where is heaven? Because sometimes I feel like she is still here with me *and* in heaven. And sometimes Steven feels like she is with him at a similar time to when I feel like she is with me – I don't mean like a ghost, I mean like a feeling, inside. Anyway, these are mysteries to be revealed at another time, I'm sure.' He smiled and took a big glug of his tea.

'You were upset when you found out the house was for sale, weren't you?'

'Yeah,' said Jim, rubbing his hair in mild embarrassment. 'I was just so used to knowing I could drop by after school... I was so scared of starting high school and everything, but Mrs Florence changed all of that. It felt like a safe place, that's all, somewhere I could go...' Jim's voice trailed off and he looked down at the carpet. There was a moment where neither of them spoke, but Jim could hear Mr Florence's breath going in and out of his nose.

'Jim,' he said finally, then waited for Jim to look up from the floor and meet his eye. 'You don't need a safe place anymore.' He stood up and moved over to Jim's chair. 'Your safe place is in here.' And he punctuated his last words with two sharp pokes of his finger to Jim's chest. 'Faith in your heart – that's your safe place.' His words seemed to break through; faith was his safe place. It was what Mrs Florence had taught him all along.

'Now,' said Mr Florence, turning towards the kitchen. 'I have to start cooking dinner. You are welcome to join us if you'd like to?'

'I had better get home Mr Fl – Bob,' Jim said. 'But thanks.' He picked up his school bag and began moving towards the door.

'Call by any time Jim, you know that.'

'Will do. See you.'

That night, after dinner had been eaten and homework had been completed, Jim sat down with a pen and paper. He considered carefully what Mr Florence had said to him and decided he needed to do something to remind himself that faith was always his safe place. He had a copy of the Lord's Prayer which was part of a worksheet they had used in an RE lesson, and he decided to use that as a basis for his own prayer to the Universe. He looked at each line of the Lord's Prayer, one at a time, and contemplated its meaning. Slowly and surely, he penned his own prayer, crafting every phrase with the precision of a poet.

When he was finished, he read it back and was satisfied. He slipped it into his school bag; he would save it for a special occasion.

Chapter Eighteen

It didn't take long for Mr Florence to sell their house. It was a popular part of Gildstow, with easy access to the main road leading to the larger town of Gippesmarket for work, but also very close to the high school, so perfect for families. And because Mr Florence and Steven were going to stay with their family in New Zealand, they didn't need to worry about waiting to buy a house out there before they moved.

It was a Saturday at the end of November when Jim went round to help them pack all of their things; they were due to fly on Sunday night, and the new owners would be moving in during the first week in December. Both parties wanted to be settled by Christmas. Jim found himself being swept up in the excitement of it all. It was a new beginning for them, and while he wasn't the one moving to New Zealand, it was a new beginning for him too.

'Take anything you want,' Mr Florence had told him as they were clearing out the living room. 'If you want any of these ornaments, or any of Eva's books, you can have them.' Jim thanked him, but he decided not to take anything. He felt he didn't need to.

Gradually the home became a house. Bigger furniture like chairs, sofas and beds had been given away; it was a collection of empty rooms, piled high with cardboard boxes.

'It seems a bit strange with nothing in it, doesn't it?' said Steven as he brought another box from upstairs into the living room.

'Yeah,' said Jim, staring from one wall to another without purpose. 'But then,' he said, 'I guess we couldn't have any beginnings if we didn't have any endings.' And he smiled at Mr Florence, who winked back at him.

'Ha!' said Steven. 'Yeah, I guess you are right there.' Jim had noticed how his face had changed since the funeral. It seemed in some way younger now, less strained. Mr Florence, too, had appeared to become rejuvenated over the weekend, as if in clearing out the house he was relieving himself of a weight he was carrying.

'Ahh,' said Mr Florence, putting another box on the pile. 'Never get too much stuff Jim, that's my advice.'

'No?' Jim asked.

'No. It just fills a space and then you hardly ever use it. Right chaps,' he said, extending his hand to both of them in turn to celebrate a job well done. 'I think we are all finished. Let's get a pizza.'

That evening, they sat around on boxes in the living room, eating takeaway pizza and chatting. Mr Florence told them stories of when they first bought the house, and how it had changed over the years.

They laughed as he told them about Steven's antics as a toddler, how he managed to lock them out of the house one day and Mr Florence had to unlock the door with a coat hanger through the letterbox. It was a family home, Mr Florence told them, and always would be.

Jim asked what was going to happen to the shop, and he said he had sold it to a man who wanted to turn it into a tattoo parlour. 'I'm not sure how well a tattoo parlour will fit in on the high street of Gildstow,' he laughed. 'But he was keen to buy the shop, so I sold it to him.'

It was gone nine o'clock before Jim realised that he should go home. Steven and Mr Florence said they would walk with him. 'It's no bother,' said Steven. 'We fancy a walk round the place before we leave anyway.'

It was a cold but cloudless night. The stars twinkled in the night sky as if they had come out to wish the Florences a fond farewell. They took the slightly longer route down to the high street and along, past the old florist shop, and then headed up to Jim's house. No other soul was around. As they walked by the buildings, old and new, Steven and Mr Florence narrated other events from their past: that was where Steven came off his bike; this was where Mrs Florence went into labour with Becky; that was where Becky had her sixteenth birthday party. And as they told each story, Jim could picture the scene so vividly in his mind that here, in this still, still moment he felt as if the past and the present were somehow blurring together, as if the three of them were somehow held outside of time and looking in on it.

When they arrived at Jim's house, Mr Florence presented Jim with a gift. 'It's not much,' he said, 'and I know you said that you didn't want anything, but I thought you might like this one.'

'Thank you,' said Jim. He held out his hand and shook both of theirs. 'Safe journey to New Zealand. Good luck with it and everything.'

They smiled and said thank you and goodbye, and then they were gone. Jim watched them leave; they put their arms around each other as the bittersweet joy of nostalgia swept over them and bonded them together.

Upstairs in his bedroom, he opened the present. It was a framed photograph of Mrs Florence. The frame itself was wooden, decorated with engravings of different flowers, and inside the frame Mrs Florence sat on her chair in the living room, smiling. She wore her large round glasses, a purple jumper and grey trousers, and the way she looked at the camera made Jim feel as if she were looking right through it and straight at him. It was just as he had imagined her in his mind the day he found out that the house was being sold. He placed the photograph on his bookcase, next to the candleholder that he had made in his art lessons.

The next day Jim woke early (or at least early for a schoolboy on a Sunday). It was one of those wakings-up where you immediately feel awake and know there is no chance of going back to sleep. As soon as he opened his eyes, an idea sprung into his mind, that he would go to the cemetery to visit Mrs Florence's grave, taking some flowers with him.

He got up and went downstairs for breakfast. 'Morning, you're up early!' said Mum as he went into the kitchen. 'After that long day you had yesterday,' she continued.

'Yeah,' replied Jim. 'I just woke up and couldn't go back to sleep, so I decided to get up.'

Mum made Jim a full English breakfast, a treat for even a Sunday morning. 'Considering all the hard work you did for Mr Florence yesterday.'

'Ahh wow, thanks Mum!'

Jim guzzled it down at such a pace that Mum asked him whether it had 'touched the sides', a phrase that he had never really understood the meaning of.

Having brushed his teeth and put his clothes on, he left the house, and headed towards the town centre. He found it funny that the one day he was going to buy flowers was a day after the one flower shop in town had closed for good; he would have to buy something less well-arranged from the local supermarket. When he got there he found a bunch of carnations in a range of pinks and chose them. He found a second bunch of a similar nature, deciding to give those to his mum.

He headed towards the edge of town where a bridge crossed the hushed and passive river and a collection of aged Tudor houses rested on the corner of a bend that led up to the cemetery, past the cricket ground. His brother, who was a huge fan of cricket, played here most weekends during the summer, but, now that the days were shorter and colder, it had become silent and lifeless once more.

At this point the road began to incline, gently at first, and then with greater intensity. By the time one reached the entrance to the cemetery on the left hand side, one was breathless and fatigued, though also blessed with a panoramic view of the whole town. Jim paused here for a moment and looked out across Gildstow, its mix of ancient and modern buildings returning to him once more a feeling of being paused somehow in time.

Just on the inside of the entrance to the graveyard was an old building with a spire, the caretaker's house, a perfect setting for some kind of ghost movie. As he walked along the path he passed old gravestones on his left, so old that they tilted to one side, as if tired and about to lie down. Even their names had disappeared, like a person without a face, the words weathered away by rain over time. No one now knew who they belonged to, their loved ones, too, buried somewhere further up.

Jim headed deeper into the cemetery, turning right towards the newer graves, where the path began to incline further and the view of Gildstow became even more spectacular. He noticed as he looked round how the town had hills on all sides, as if it were built inside of a hole.

He found the youngest graves, with the grassy mounds in front of each wooden cross still bulging out, like a long row of pregnant women lying on the ground. The graves were in their infancy, too young to hold the weight of a headstone, and were marked with a crucifix instead.

Jim found the date of death on each one, starting with the most recent, and then tracked back until he found what he was looking for. When he reached Mrs Florence's grave, he realised he could have guessed it was hers, for it was already adorned with an array of stunning flowers, a rainbow of petals, a parting gift from husband and son.

Jim decided to separate his bunch out and found small gaps to insert each pink carnation. When done, he stood up and looked at the grave. It seemed an odd thing to do now that he was here; after everything he had felt about Mrs Florence it seemed wrong to imagine that this was where she was. Yet he knew, in his heart, that really she wasn't there, she was with the Universe. Nonetheless, it was nice to have a place to visit.

'I wrote this,' he said to the grave, the flowers and the air, pulling a crumpled piece of paper out of his pocket. 'And I wanted to read it to you.' He paused for a moment and then continued. 'It's my prayer to the Universe, my own Lord's Prayer I guess.'

Again he paused, feeling a little bit silly talking like this in an open space with no one around. Yet he definitely felt he was talking to someone. He unfolded his piece of paper and began to read it as if he were nervously delivering a speech in front of his class.

'Dear Universe,' he said. 'let me always follow your path, to be in the right place at the right time. Give me the things that I need today and forgive me for the things I do wrong. I know that each and every day is a success and that faith is my safe place. I see that each ending leads to a new beginning and I accept each one without fear. My fear evaporates into nothing, because you give me all that I need.'

He folded the paper up, stood and waited. The flowers stayed the same; the clouds stayed the same; nothing seemed to change. The wind continued to offer a gentle breeze. He said goodbye to Mrs Florence and began to walk back down the hill and towards the exit of the cemetery. With each step the gravestones grew older and older until he passed the faceless ones once more and stepped out onto the main road.

Nothing outside of him had changed. And yet, as he took each step, one at a time, he felt within himself a rising joy, a growing light, much like he had felt at Mrs Florence's funeral. As he headed down past the cricket ground and the ancient Tudor houses, over the placid river and back towards home, he felt the joy fill his body, all the way to his head, and he couldn't help but smile. He passed some parishioners on the way home from the morning service at the church, elderly couples gently following tradition, and they looked at him strangely, this boy with a broad grin across his face. But he didn't mind.

'Morning!' he said gleefully as he passed.

'Oh,' one of them would say in surprise, and then 'Good morning to you!' And smiles would spread contagiously across their faces.

When he got home, his mum was still in the kitchen. 'I got you some flowers Mum!' he said, handing her the bunch of carnations.

'Oh, they're lovely, thank you Jim!' and she kissed him on the cheek.

'Do you fancy doing something today?'

'Oh,' said Mum, surprised at being asked to do something by her son. 'Yes I think that would be a really nice idea.'

'Ok, great, I'll just go and ask John and Dad!' And he walked out of the kitchen to find his brother and father as his mother watched him with a bemused smile on her face.

The family did go out that day, and it was one of the happiest family days that Jim could remember. They headed up to the coast, walked along the beach and had lunch in a nearby pub. Jim's cheerfulness was a tsunami that washed through all of them. Nothing, not the petty arguments between his mum and dad, not John's teenage annoyance at having to spend Sunday with his family rather than his girlfriend, could survive the flood; all that was left was happiness. It seemed, as they walked along the beach, that the clouds themselves were driven away revealing an infinite blue sky and a golden winter sun.

'This was a brilliant idea Jim,' said Mum. 'What a lovely day out!'

The next day Jim's glee had calmed down somewhat. He said his prayer to the Universe in the morning, the first thing he did after getting out of bed, and instead of being overwhelmed with cheerfulness he felt happily contented.

The day went by smoothly; algebra with Mrs Numbers, sketching with Mr Ronald, poetry with Mr Simpson and Vikings with Mr Ashoka. He looked for opportunities to help others wherever he could, to recognise their successes in their daily lives and spread his own feeling of happiness. He just did little things, but they all had a positive effect: he told the boy on the table opposite him that he thought his sketch was really good in art; he told the lady in the canteen how much he liked her macaroni cheese; and he told a girl working in the same group as him in maths that she had managed to solve an algebra puzzle far quicker than he had.

The bell went for the end of school and Jim started to walk home. He met his brother and Jennifer at the school gates.

'Alright Jim, walking home?' said John.

'Hiya, yeah I am.'

'Great, we'll walk with you.'

'Ok, cool.'

Jim found this unusual. 'How come you're walking this way?'

'Jennifer's coming round ours for dinner tonight.'

'Ahh cool. It'll be good to have another player for PremierFoot Soccer.'

'Mmm, we probably won't play PremierFoot Soccer Jim,' said his brother.

'Why not?' said Jennifer with fake indignation. 'I love PremierFoot Soccer! We play it all the time round our house Jim. John probably doesn't want to play because he doesn't want to get beaten by his girlfriend in front of his brother,' she said teasingly.

Jim laughed while John attempted to filibuster. 'That's not true Jen, I just thought you might not like to play computer games all evening. You might like to get to know my parents and stuff.'

They had reached the top of Black Hill and Jim was surprised to see Lucy, the girl he sat next to in his English lessons, loitering at the entrance to the alleyway.

'Hi Lucy,' he said.

'Hi,' she replied. Jim observed on her face an emotion that he was all too familiar with – worry. It seemed as if she didn't want to be there, but was nonetheless anchored to that spot. He told his brother and Jennifer that he would catch them up and went over to Lucy.

'Thanks for your help in English again today,' he said. 'I'm not sure I'd understand William Blake without you.'

'That's alright,' she said. 'My mum's a big fan of William Blake. She can say large chunks of him off by heart. I've probably been listening to his poems since

I was a baby.' Even as she spoke, she was looking around, shifting her bag from one shoulder to the next, as if she were uncomfortable to be there, anxious to move on.

'Wow, I don't think my parents have ever quoted poetry at me.' Lucy made an attempt to laugh, then there was an awkward pause.

Jim decided to dive in with his question. 'Erm, I hope you don't mind me asking Lucy, but are you ok?'

She looked up at him and her eyes looked as if they might burst with tears at any moment. It seemed as if she was now caught between the worry of telling Jim what was wrong, and appearing foolish, and the worry of what was actually wrong.

Eventually she spoke, but continued to look around rather than meet his eyes with her own. 'Ahh, well,' she said. 'The thing is, I have to walk down here to get home, and I've heard the rumours about Black Hill, and... I'm a bit scared about going down there.' Now that she had spoken she searched Jim's face for any sign of ridicule, but she found none.

'That's fair enough,' said Jim, nodding. 'I felt exactly the same the first few times I had to walk down here. Come on, I'm going this way anyway. We can walk together.'

A slight look of uncertainty still occupied Lucy's brow, but the news that she would have a companion for her journey eased much of her worry. They walked slowly down the hill, steep as it was and cautious as Lucy was, but Jim did not mind, for he liked Lucy.

'Did you really feel scared the first time you came down here?' Lucy asked.

'Yeah definitely. The first few times actually.'

'That surprises me.'

'Why?'

'You always seem so brave in class.'

Jim couldn't help letting out a little laugh. 'Sorry,' he said. 'It's just I've never really thought of myself as brave before.' And he hadn't, because when he realised that the Universe was there to help him whenever he needed it, it wasn't a matter of courage so much as a matter of faith. 'I think it's just that I've learnt something this first term at high school.'

'What's that?'

'We have nothing to fear but fear itself.'

'That sounds very poetic.'

'Well, it's from a book – To Kill a Mockingbird, but other people have said similar things before. Sir Francis Bacon, President Roosevelt.' Jim had done some research.

'Who are all these people?' Lucy asked, impressed.

'If I'm honest, I don't really know, but I sounded clever, didn't I?'

'Yeah, I guess you did,' said Lucy, and she laughed. 'We have nothing to fear but fear itself. I like that.'

'Yeah.'

They reached the bottom of the hill and turned into the alleyway when Lucy cried out. Jim turned to see that her school bag had broken and its contents had spilled onto the ground. 'Ohh!' she said, as they both bent down to pick things up. 'This bag has been falling apart for ages. Mum kept saying that she would buy me a new one after we moved house. Now she is going to have to.' Lucy held up her bag for Jim to inspect; it was a ruin, a casualty of having to carry too many school books. Strategically placed safety pins attempted to hold parts of the bag together, but to no avail.

'You've just moved house?' asked Jim.

'Yeah, it's why I have to walk down Black Hill now. Come on, I'll show you.' Carrying the contents of her school bag in her arms, she walked ahead of Jim and exited the alleyway of Black Hill onto Mrs Florence's road. For a moment Jim stayed where he was. Surely, he thought, it couldn't be. He followed Lucy out with urgency to find her standing on Mrs Florence's lawn, in front of Mrs Florence's house.

'Here it is!' She said. 'Why do you look so surprised?' For a look of sheer wonder had spread over Jim's face.

'Oh, it's just…' he began. 'I knew the people that lived here before.'

'Oh really? How strange!' Lucy replied. 'Thanks for helping me with my stuff.'

'That's alright.'

'Would you like to come in for a snack? I think Mum has got some custard creams in the cupboard.'

A broad smile came across Jim's face at the magic of the Universe. 'Yes please, that would be great.'

Inside, the house was already beginning to change. Lucy's dad was in the dining room applying an undercoat of white paint; Lucy's mum was in the kitchen unpacking their belongings. They both greeted Jim with a friendly smile when Lucy introduced him. Lucy's mum gave them a plate of custard creams and suggested they do something useful, so they began to unpack things in the living room.

When Jim realised that it was four o'clock he said that he had to leave, but they agreed to meet at the top of Black Hill the next day to walk down together again. As he made his way home, he couldn't keep the smile from his face. The Universe, he thought, was a wondrous thing to move his life on in this way. He had never had a friend who was a girl before and he found that he quite liked the idea of it. When he remembered Lucy's bag falling apart, he couldn't help but think of a young Mr and Mrs Florence, meeting for the first time on the platform at Paddington station.

He turned the corner that led to his road and walked up to the drive. Inside his house, Mum was attempting to win Jennifer's favour by offering her lots of cake. He thought about the conversation he had had with Lucy.

'Do you like your new house?' Jim had asked as they were unpacking a box of books and placing them on the bookcase.

'It's ok,' she replied. 'I heard there was an old witch that used to live here.'

'Oh no,' Jim replied. 'I wouldn't have called her a witch, but she definitely knew magic.'

Lucy looked at him as if he were trying to make fun of her. 'How did you know her?' she asked.

'She was my friend.'

'I think I preferred my old house,' Lucy said after a respectful pause. 'It was more in the countryside. I'm a bit sad to leave that all behind.'

'That's fair enough,' Jim said. ' But then,' he continued, 'you couldn't have any beginnings if you didn't have any endings.'

33195722R00117

Printed in Poland
by Amazon Fulfillment
Poland Sp. z o.o., Wrocław